THE PEACOCK HOUSE

Tania Jordan loved her work as a successful interior designer. She didn't need her sister Ellie to find her a suitable partner. Harry Fitzroy had been the only man for her. And Harry was dead. Then Luke Sinclair — a name she'd tried hard to forget — came back into her life. And he'd bought The Peacock House, the Fitzroy family home — and he wanted Tania to do the makeover.

Books by Clare Tyler
in the Linford Romance Library:

NEVER SAY GOODBYE

CLARE TYLER

THE PEACOCK HOUSE

Complete and Unabridged

LINFORD
Leicester

First published in Great Britain in 2001

First Linford Edition
published 2004

The moral right of the author has been asserted

This is a work of fiction. Names and characters are the product of the author's imagination and any resemblance to any actual persons, living or dead, is purely coincidental.

British Library CIP Data

Tyler, Clare
    The Peacock House.—Large print ed.—
Linford romance library
    1. Women interior decorators—England—Fiction
    2. Love stories 3. Large type books
    I. Title
    823.9'14 [F]

    ISBN 1–84395–421–4

Published by
F. A. Thorpe (Publishing)
Anstey, Leicestershire

Set by Words & Graphics Ltd.
Anstey, Leicestershire
Printed and bound in Great Britain by
T. J. International Ltd., Padstow, Cornwall

This book is printed on acid-free paper

1

The telephone rang. It was Ellie.

'Tania?' The voice was high and brisk with excitement.

Tania had been sipping her Friday night glass of Chardonnay. She liked to unwind at the end of the week, shoes off, wine and Mozart. It had become a ritual with her.

Recently, she'd feared that she might be sinking into a rut with her 'singleton' habits, but then she decided that she was entitled to live her life how she wanted — she was going for it her way and blow everyone else. Which was why she dreaded her younger sister's telephone calls. She loved Ellie as much as anybody could love a sister, but Ellie had one overriding character flaw. She was bossy! Happily married to commodity broker Charles Wainwright, she was forever trying to mate Tania with suitable male partners.

'Hello darling.' Tania turned down the CD player, hoping that Ellie wasn't going to make a session of it or, worse still, issue a dinner party invitation for tonight. Tania was looking forward to a pasta supper on a tray and that Oscar-winning video which she'd at last managed to hire from the corner shop. 'How are Charles and the boys?'

'They're fine. I've just met a man,' Ellie said, coming straight to the point. Tania's heart sank. They'd been down this route many times. It always ended in words. 'Last night actually, at a dinner party. Very high-powered, with looks to die for.' The purr in Ellie's voice was unmistakable. Tania's heart sank even further.

'I can't . . . ' Her excuse was cut off before it had got going.

'Guess what?'

'I can't imagine,' Tania said wryly and waited patiently. It was no use trying to interrupt Ellie once she was in full flow. Experience had taught Tania

2

that it was best to sit things out. Mentally, she began planning her next job.

'He's bought The Peacock House.'

Jerked back to the present, Tania clutched the receiver so hard that it hurt her hand. Her heartbeat did a quick military tattoo.

'Peacock — as in 'Peacock' . . . ?' She asked, hoping that her voice sounded normal. Her body certainly didn't feel normal. A glance in the mirror showed her eyes which were double pools of aquamarine in a face drained of colour. It had happened ten years ago, but it seemed like yesterday.

Ellie bubbled with laughter, unaware of the impact of her words on her sister. 'Peacock, as in 'Peacock',' she confirmed. 'Remember it?' How could Tania forget? She swayed. Ellie had only been eleven at the time. She wouldn't remember — but Tania did. 'Isn't it amazing?'

'Amazing,' Tania echoed faintly, then switched off. She was still having trouble controlling her heartbeat. It was silly to feel like this after all this time. She should have outgrown her emotions and memories. They belonged to the past and The Peacock House hadn't been a part of her life for more years than she cared to remember.

If she closed her eyes, she could see it now. Bathed in evening sunlight at the end of a beautiful summer's day — the country retreat of the aristocratic stockbroking Fitzroy family. It had been built in the 1920's — elegant, comfortable, and named after the peacocks that used to roam freely in the grounds. Strutting across the manicured lawns, flaunting jade and turquoise plumes, the fine birds were synonymous in many ways with the Fitzroys. They, too, were handsome and proud — and they knew it — and how they'd strutted!

By the time that Tania had met Harry, the house had passed through several generations of Fitzroys. Harry was the last of the line and due to inherit. She hadn't thought about

Harry for a long time — she'd programmed herself not to. Even now it hurt too much to remember but he still held a special place in her heart. He'd had more than his fair share of character flaws, but she'd accepted them and loved him all the same. In her memory, he was forever young and beautiful. He'd been taken from her before life had been given a chance to corrupt him.

For a long time after Harry, there'd been no one in her life. Then she'd had the occasional relationship but, somehow, no one had ever taken his place. She knew that it was silly to feel like this after so long, and for someone like Harry Fitzroy who hadn't been ready to settle down. But, she couldn't help herself and she certainly couldn't explain it to Ellie, who'd never experienced the slightest emotional hiccup in her well-ordered life. Charles Wainwright was as different from Harry Fitzroy as it was possible to be. And he adored Ellie.

'Tania? Are you still there? Or am I talking to myself?'

Ellie's voice jump-started Tania back to the present. 'Sorry Ellie.' Tania cleared her throat. 'Your news took me by surprise, that's all. Fancy you remembering The Peacock House.'

Tania turned her back on the wall mirror. She'd never been vain, but even she was convinced that her reflection couldn't look that peculiar.

'You used to go on about it all the time.'

'Did I?' Ellie's words sent a ripple of shock through her system. There was so much she still didn't remember.

'Yes, you did.' Tania could hear the amusement in Ellie's voice. Clearly there were no skeletons in the cupboard of her memory of The Peacock House.

After Harry's accident, Ellie had been packed off to relatives in Cornwall and Tania, just wanting to get away, had moved to London. By the time Ellie had grown up, their parents were dead and The Peacock House was just a golden memory of happier days. Life had moved on.

Tania had been Ellie's senior bridesmaid when she'd made a brilliant marriage at the age of eighteen and gone on dutifully, less than a year later, to produce cherubic twin boys. Having got the fundamentals out the way, she'd then made it her life's challenge to see her sister married off — so far without success. It had been the one failure in Ellie's charmed life and Tania suspected that it irked her sister.

'There was a bit about the sale in one of the glossy mags.' Ellie was talking about The Peacock House again. 'I've cut it out for you. The Fitzroys sold up years ago and it had fallen into neglect before Luke Sinclair bought it. He wants to do it up. Return it to its original state.'

Tania made an effort to concentrate on what Ellie was saying.

'Do we know anything about this Luke Sinclair?' she asked.

'Charles has put out feelers, but

without much success so far. Apparently he's a businessman and tired of crossing the Atlantic all the time. He's English, but lived in the United States for years — something to do with computers. He wants a permanent base back in England and The Peacock House came on the market at just the right time. It's been empty for ages. The market was depressed, then a sale fell through — all that sort of thing.'

'I see.'

'He was very keen to tell me all about it, especially when I told him we'd lived in the area. Not that I remembered much about it of course. It was always more your scene . . . '

Tania sipped some wine. It still hurt her throat to swallow. The Peacock House and its inhabitants had long since ceased to be a part of her life. There was no need for her to feel like a squeezed-out wreck. Then why did she? She must pull herself together. She glanced at her watch. It had been hours since she'd eaten. She'd get rid of Ellie, have her supper, then veg out on the sofa with the rest of the wine and the video.

Only . . . Tania had never been one for intuitions or sixth senses, but tonight the hairs on the back of her neck seemed to be doing funny things. She had a premonition that something was about to happen — something she wasn't going to like. She didn't have to wait very long for her fears to come true.

'*And* he's looking for someone to do the interior design.' Ellie couldn't disguise the triumph in her voice.

'That'll be quite a job I should imagine. Thinking of offering your services?' Tania asked with a laugh. She should have known better.

'No. I offered yours.' The reply ricocheted back down the line.

It took Tania a moment or two to absorb their meaning.

'You did . . . what?' she asked, not sure that she had heard Ellie correctly.

'He said he'd heard of your work

through a business connection. You did someone's house somewhere and they recommended you.' Ellie sounded a bit vague. 'Anyway, the buzz is that he wants you. Isn't that brilliant? And on my say so. I did an amazing sales job on you, Tania, so don't let me down.'

'You had no right Ellie . . . '

'Of course I did. You undersell yourself. Look at that work you did for that junior government minister. His wife was over the moon! You never did push that pitch to its full sales potential.'

'I only purchased a couple of paintings for them.'

'So? That's a form of interior design, isn't it?'

'It's not the same thing at all. Besides, Ellie . . . ' Tania decided it was time to be firm, 'I like to organise my own professional life. I have to meet clients before I decide whether or not we can work together.'

That much was true. Tania had to have an empathy with her customers, otherwise things didn't work. If they didn't like her, or she didn't feel she was the right person for them, then no amount of persuasion could change her mind. Ellie knew this. What on earth had possessed her to interfere? It would be embarrassing explaining things to this Mr Sinclair. There were times when Tania felt like strangling her sister — and right now was one of them. She'd meddled too far this time.

'It will look good on your CV.' Ellie continued unabashed. 'Think what it could lead to. You need to get out and about. Always stuck in London, working for city types. Where's the challenge in that? The Peacock House is perfect, a complete change of direction. You need to diversify. You're not fulfilling your development potential.'

In any other circumstances, Tania would have burst out laughing. To hear Ellie, who'd never had a proper job in her life, spouting on about 'development potential', was absolutely priceless. But this was no laughing matter. Ellie didn't seem to realise the enormity of what she'd done. It was time for some straight talking.

'Ellie, I am perfectly satisfied with things the way they are. I don't need you organising my life — professional or social.'

The rebuke was wasted on Ellie.

'You're getting middle-aged before your time; stuck in a rut. You don't want to be a spinster all your life. You need a lifestyle change, a make-over . . . '

'Ellie, will you stop talking nonsense? I'm quite happy as I am.'

'A bit of fresh country air. You know that you always loved the Cotswolds. Retrace your roots and treat it as a spring break. That part of the world will be looking lovely at this time of year.'

Taking a spring break was absolutely the last thing Tania wanted to do. Besides, The Peacock House had always looked lovely, whatever the season: in winter sunlight, on frosty days, summer evenings and spring afternoons. So, she didn't need to see it in all the glory of a full-blown daffodil-laden spring.

She heard muffled voices down the line.

'Can't stop, Tania. We're going to the theatre. Charles is champing at the bit, but I had to call you and let you know the good news. Let's do lunch next week? It's ages since I've been to town.'

'Ellie, listen to me. I can't . . . '

'Whoops. So excited I nearly forgot to give you the details. Hold on. His name's Luke Sinclair. But I've told you that already, haven't I? Now, where did I put my notes?'

'Yes. Give me the contact number. I'll call him back.' Tania began hunting round for a pad and pencil. It would be no good relying on Ellie to do it.

Through a haze which was threatening to become a headache, she could hear Ellie searching around down the other end of the line, 'Here we are. Next Tuesday. Eleven o'clock. The Peacock House, Little Chipping. He asked you not to be late, because he's

13

flying off later to America. I told him that you'd be there — and that you're never late.'

'Ellie,' Tania's voice rose on a high note, 'One of us will have to ring Luke Sinclair back and explain that I don't . . . '

'Coming darling,' Ellie called to Charles. 'Gotta go, Tania. Let me know how you get on. I'll keep my fingers crossed for you. Good luck. Not that you need it.'

'Ellie — his number . . . ?'

But Tania found herself talking to a disconnected line.

* * *

Tania sipped her coffee in The Feathers and ran through her brief notes. It had been a pointless exercise making any, of course, but to her surprise she'd enjoyed the experience. She had no precise idea of what Luke Sinclair was looking for, but she had a few concepts which she knew would work. Not that she was going to take the commission, of course, but she'd decided it would be unprofessional to turn up for the appointment totally unprepared.

She glanced down at her watch, glad that her early start had left her with time to spare. Once she'd left the motorway and the scenery had softened into mellow stone, she'd felt the weight of London slipping from her shoulders.

She had forgotten how different the air smelt in the Cotswolds. Smiling, she'd wound down her window, allowing the May sunshine to invade the stuffiness of her hired hatchback as she'd driven slowly through villages — no more than a clutch of cottages alongside rushing streams, which years ago had powered the mills in their wool-producing heyday. Clumps of cow parsley slumbered on the grassy banks and deep pink foxgloves had bowed their top-heavy heads as she passed.

Little Chipping nestled in a forgotten valley alongside a small tributary of The Leach. It boasted a mill, a medieval English church, a village green with a water trough and The Feathers Inn. The village was deeply unfashionable with the long lines of coaches and tourists, who poured daily into the larger and more developed neighbouring villages. Forgotten by time, it nestled unnoticed in its quiet corner of golden radiance, a jewel known only to a few.

Tania paid for her coffee and went outside into the sharp brilliance of the morning. She decided to leave her car at The Feathers and walk the rest of the way. The ground looked a bit damp still from the showery spring weather, and not totally suited to her footwear, but the fresh air would clear her head and she needed to stretch her legs after the long drive.

She knew the way like the back of her hand. A gentle stroll of twenty minutes should be enough to reach The Peacock House in good time for the punctual Luke Sinclair — whom she knew that she was going to dislike on sight. It wasn't his fault that she was in this mess, of course. But, she felt an irrational antipathy towards a man who could engage an interior designer, merely on the recommendation of an enthusiastic sister. Where was the business acumen in that? She hoped that he ran his business empire with more efficiency than he seemed to have displayed so far.

She'd tried ringing Ellie all weekend. However, despite leaving numerous messages, her sister hadn't rung back — on purpose, Tania suspected. She'd definitely be having words with Ellie when she got back to London. This interference in her life simply *had* to stop!

Only her professional integrity, since she didn't want to get a reputation for unreliability — a death knell in the cut-throat world of interior design — together with an almost overwhelming curiosity to see the house, once again, had forced her to keep the appointment.

Tania took a deep breath. The air was as soft as silk. She walked slowly, savouring the spring delights of the day. Very little had changed since she had last been here. In fact, she suspected that very little had changed in Little Chipping for the last three hundred years. The terrace of cottages still hugged the dusty path which bordered the stream.

Standing on the rickety footbridge, she looked down at the fish cutting scarlet swathes through the clear water. She and Harry used to stand on this very bridge and share their dreams. Caught up in her reverie, it took Tania a moment or two to realise that the much larger, quick flash of scarlet at the corner of her eye, wasn't actually a fish, but a high performance Italian car.

It appeared to be moving very carefully along the riverside path, its muted exhaust muffled as it edged its way past the church and the water trough. Even from behind the tinted windscreen, Tania could feel the driver's eyes on her.

It was probably fair to say that in her blue business suit, crisply tailored blouse and high heels, she might look a bit out of place. But the uniform went with the job. She also liked to wear her thick chestnut hair up in a neat pleat. It sent out a message which she hoped gave customers confidence in her efficiency.

The car eased round the bend and Tania caught her first glimpse of the driver. Like her, he was dressed for business in a white shirt and grey suit. The only jar on her senses was his tie. From where she stood, it looked like a giant yellow sunflower.

Blinking in surprise, she took an involuntary step backwards and tee- tered as her heels lost their hold on the footbridge. She clutched her briefcase to her chest and made a grab for the handrail — before she remembered there wasn't one.

Arms flailing wildly, she knew that she looked ridiculous and suddenly found herself feeling annoyed. The sun was warm and she could feel her blouse sticking to her back as she steadied herself, finally managing to stop impersonating a windmill. Maybe it hadn't been a good idea to walk to the house, after all?

A furious, crimson flush stained her cheeks as Tania saw the Ferrari driver's lips twitching in amusement as she struggled to regain control of her dignity. The car slid effortlessly to a halt and the passenger window eased down. She would have taken another step backwards if it had been possible, but that really would have meant ending up in the stream.

'Can I help you?' she asked in a suitably impersonal voice. He was probably some business type who'd taking a wrong turning. Hay carts rather than Ferraris were the more usual mode of transport in Little Chipping.

'Miss Jordan?' The voice was deep, the eyes blue and the lips were still curved with amusement.

Tania's heart began to thump erratically. It couldn't be him! But who else would know her name in Little Chipping? Their rented cottage had been in the next village and no one would remember her now.

'I'm afraid you have the advantage of me.' She knew that she sounded pompous, but she hoped her words would wipe the laughter from his eyes.

To her horror, Tania could feel the edge of the footbridge, which had clearly been eroded by the winter weather, beginning to crumble under her feet. She'd have to get off it fast, if she didn't want to wind up in the bubbling stream below, but this scarlet monster and grinning driver were barring her way.

'Luke Sinclair,' he replied easily. 'Glad to see that you're on time for our appointment.'

Tania gave a slight whimper as her Italian leather shoes slid sideways.

'I think you'd better get in the car, don't you?'

The dimple in his chin deepened as he opened the door for her. From where she was standing, Tania could smell the upholstery. Further movement beneath her feet quickly convinced her that it wasn't a time for dignity or expensive smells.

'Thank you.'

She cleared the space between them in one rather unladylike leap, and found herself almost flat on her back in a low-slung car seat, looking up at a man whose eyes were brimming with unmistakable laughter as he took in her now rather grubby blouse and laddered tights.

As he leant across her to close the door, Tania flattened herself further back into the seat. She couldn't have made a worse start if she had tried! A soft chestnut curl stroked her ear and she realised that her hair was also falling apart — along with her control of the situation.

'There, that's better, isn't it?' The blue eyes smiled down into hers. Tania wasn't short, but having squashed herself down in the seat in her frantic attempt not to come into contact with Luke Sinclair's tanned flesh, she found that he was now towering over her.

She didn't like playing 'the little woman' — or being an object of ridicule, for that matter.

'Thank you.' Her voice caught in her throat as she struggled to straighten up. The creature was actually enjoying the situation, although she totally failed to see what was so funny.

'Unless you know them,' he said conversationally, 'these old village foot-bridges can be lethal. I remember once . . . '

'Thank you,' she repeated, adding, 'I have been here before and I am familiar with village footbridges.'

'Are you? I thought you looked a bit lost just now, as if you didn't really know what you were doing here.'

Tania bit her lip. He must have caught her daydreaming about Harry. She tossed her head and the curl tickled her ear again. How dared this man, Luke Sinclair, patronise her? She knew this village better than he did. It wasn't her fault that the bridge had given way under her weight, and she'd known exactly where she was going. More than ever, she began to wish that she hadn't come. Ellie would be made to pay for this latest interference . . . with interest!

With these thoughts raging through her mind, the best retort she could come up with was, 'I lost my footing.'

'Yes, I saw that.' The amusement was back in his voice.

'You took me by surprise, coming round the corner like that.'

'I'm sorry.'

If Tania hadn't been feeling so thrown by the situation, she'd have quite liked the sound of his voice. It had the low, deep note of the softly honed Cotswold vowels, which she recalled from her childhood, she told herself, before being suddenly struck by a sudden thought. Perhaps he *was* local? Hadn't Ellie said something about him being English? Perhaps he had come back to . . .

'Shall we get on? I have a heavy schedule.' His voice, which Tania now decided she didn't like at all, sliced sharply into her thoughts.

He pressed the accelerator and the car moved gently forwards. Tania noticed the material of his elegant suit straining against his thigh as he applied pressure to the foot pedal. The action caused a strange sensation in her chest, something like a box of fluttering butterflies. She shifted uncomfortably in her seat. What on earth was the matter with her? It must be something in the Cotswold air.

'I expect you'd have lost your way, as well.'

'What?' Tania jammed the misbehaving curl behind her ear, his eyes lingering on her fingers as she fought to rearrange her hair. 'What did you say?' She raised her voice when he didn't immediately reply.

The car eased forward again as he returned his attention to the path. 'You really shouldn't have tried to walk there. The Peacock House isn't too easy to find, unless you know where you're going.'

If he was being insufferable on purpose, Tania decided that she wouldn't give him the satisfaction of rising to his bait, even if his words did set her teeth on edge. The sooner she got through with this farce of an appointment, and back to her London flat, the better. She'd already made up her mind on this one. Luke Sinclair was not a person she could work with.

'I think I could have managed to find my way there,' she managed to say, with award-winning self-control. It seemed that Ellie hadn't told him of their connection with the house. Unless of course, like Tania, he'd switched off and let Ellie do the talking.

'I presume you have a car?'

'Of course, I have!' she snapped. 'You

don't think I walked all the way from London, do you?'

She lost the battle with her self-control, roughly thrusting her recalcitrant curl behind her ear for the third time. Why was nothing following its job description today? She wasn't normally so edgy and she was more than capable of dealing with a few, minor professional setbacks. But the eyebrow he raised at the tone of her voice was the final straw.

'And I don't need you to show me the way to Little Chipping,' she added curtly. 'Or to The Peacock House, for that matter.'

She caught her breath in her chest. She knew she was being unspeakably rude, but she couldn't help herself. He was being so damn condescending — driving down here in his fancy car, lecturing her about foot-bridges, and then offering to show her the way to The Peacock House. How dare he?

She glanced away from his hands, which were making a good job of

controlling the steering wheel in difficult circumstances. The last part of the
drive wouldn't be easy, as the track
became narrower before reaching the
entrance to the house. She decided to
keep quiet, allowing him to find that
one out for himself. Besides, if they
carried on like this, they'd both wind
up in the river Leach.

She moved her briefcase off her lap,
noticing to her horror that it had left a
damp stain of dubious origin, right in
the centre of her woollen skirt. She
knew instantly that it would never come
out. Which meant that her suit was
ruined. Once again, she felt Luke
Sinclair's eyes on her.

He opened his mouth to speak, took
one look at the expression on her face,
and just smiled at her. This time, it
wasn't a smile of amusement. It was a
smile of genuine sympathy.

In a split second, years seemed to slip
from the calendar and Tania was
eighteen again — gazing into the face of
the man she loved.

'Life can sometimes be a real pain, can't it?' She heard Luke Sinclair's voice through a haze and knew that his comment referred to her skirt.

'Yes, it can,' she said. Only her reply had nothing to do with skirts, or with stains which wouldn't come out.

2

'Are we wasting our time?' Luke's voice echoed round the empty room, as Tania's heightened complexion drained to the colour of pale whitewash.

'Yes.'

Her reply snapped an involuntary '*What?*' from his lips. He wasn't sure that he'd heard her correctly. He'd been busy admiring her eyes. He'd forgotten their deep amethyst colour, and how he'd always wanted to drown in them. Even in his wildest dreams, he could never have imagined that she would grow up to be so beautiful. He loved her so much that it gave him a pain in his chest. But he mustn't let her know — not yet. That would ruin everything.

He also wanted to laugh. That ridiculous curl of chestnut hair was still bobbing up and down over her left ear, in tune with whatever emotion was turning her eyes that magical colour. He fought down an urge to pull her roughly to him and kiss the life out of her, until she begged him to stop.

He drew himself up sharply. He'd waited long enough for this moment, he mustn't blow it now — just because the very sight of Tania Jordan was threatening to dismantle his carefully engineered plans. It wasn't a time for laughter, kisses or amethyst eyes. It was a time for panic. Because, she'd just turned him down!

From the moment he'd seen her on that daft little bridge spanning the stream, dreaming about the past, he'd known. Luke had only ever loved one woman in his life — Tania Jordan. He'd thought for one moment that she'd recognised him. His lips tightened grimly. But all those years ago, she'd only ever had eyes for Harry Fitzroy.

As he'd swung the car through the wrought iron gates which had seen better days, he'd heard her make a funny little noise at the back of her throat and he'd known exactly how she'd felt. His first sight of The Peacock House after so many years had also left him feeling that he'd been punched in the gut.

She'd gone very quiet for the last part of the drive and Luke had begun to wish that he hadn't teased her. But she looked the sort that could take it. There'd never been anything of the wilting flower about Tania Jordan. Which was one of the reasons why she'd always been such fun to be with. His palms had felt damp against the steering wheel, and he'd realised that they were sweating badly. But she hadn't even noticed. In fact, he seriously doubted whether she even realised that he was sitting next to her in the car. Her eyes had been fixed solely on the house. And even though he'd seen it many times before, and in many weathers, he had to admit that it looked magnificent, nestling in the morning sunshine; a little seedy per-haps, but not beyond repair. In Luke's fast-paced world of technology, there was no room for sentiment, but even his own heartbeat had quickened at the sight and memories the house evoked.

Now they were facing each other across the bare floorboards, in what had once been the Fitzroys' elegant drawing room. And she'd just told him that they were wasting their time. He was gutted. Perhaps he should tell her everything — now?

Tania's mouth had gone suddenly dry. Coming back here had knocked her senses all over the place. She'd had no idea that it would be like this. It was as if the house had stretched out its arms, wrapping her in a loving embrace like a long lost friend . . . a friend in dire need of help.

The lawns were no longer mani-cured, windows were broken and the garden was a wilderness, but the raw material was a beckoning blank canvas. Tania couldn't even see through the picture windows leading down to the old peacock lawn, because they were so ingrained with years of Cotswold weather. But she knew — *just knew* — that this was a project which she couldn't turn down. Not even her very first, professional commission had made her feel this excited. She was so fired up, that she'd even pay Luke Sinclair for the privilege!

'It's no good.' She quite took Luke's breath away as she strode round the room. 'Mr Sinclair . . . ' She swung around on one mud-encrusted, Italian leather shoe.

'Luke.'

She hesitated, then moving her lips into a reluctant smile, inclined her head. 'Very well . . . er . . . Luke.'

The way she said his name caused his breath to catch in his chest.

'My notes are no good, because . . . ' She snatched savagely at the bobbing curl of hair and rammed it into her now seriously disorganised French pleat. As it immediately fell out again. Luke found himself longing to tuck it behind her ear for her. ' . . . It's all my sister's fault.'

Luke blinked. He'd obviously missed something. 'Your sister . . . ?

'Yes.'

'Mrs Wainright . . . ? Ellie? What fault . . . ? And what's it got to do with your sister?' He was growing more bewildered by the minute.

'Everything.' Tania looked like a child, knowing that she had to confess, but not sure what strategy to adopt. 'I'm not making any sense, am I?'

'No,' he said gently. 'But carry on. I expect that I'll pick it up as we go along.'

'I . . . I didn't want this commission.' She took a deep breath, plunging quickly on before second thoughts could stop her. 'In fact, I only came along, today, because I didn't have an address or contact phone number for you.'

Luke's lips twitched. He'd been so careful not to give any numbers to Ellie Wainwright, but it hadn't been easy.

35

Tania's sister was a powerhouse of persistence. He'd nearly blown his cover several times.

'And I didn't want to just not turn up,' Tania was saying, anxiously chewing the lipstick off her lower lip as she spoke.

Luke preferred her lips their natural pink colour. He also preferred her laddered tights and muddy shoes to the artificial creature whom he'd glimpsed in Little Chipping. This was the real Tania Jordan standing in front of him now. The flesh and blood one, fired by enthusiasm, embarrassed as she stumbled through an explanation which he didn't really want to hear.

'So, I thought that I'd better make a few token notes — just to show willing.'

'Token notes are for people who have no taste and aren't really interested in interior design — just as long as it costs a fortune?' he forced himself to drawl. If he was too eager at this stage, he could kill the whole thing stone dead. 'You put me in that bracket, do you?'

'No, of course, not.'

'Sounds like it to me.'

'You don't understand!' Luke had taken off his jacket and Tania would have liked to remove her own. But she feared that her blouse might be slightly transparent, and she really didn't want to give Luke Sinclair's eyes any more ammunition. He was far too perceptive as it was.

He was now looking at her with ... Tania couldn't quite identify that strange gleam in his eyes. It was almost ... well, almost as if he knew her. But that was ridiculous, since she was quite certain that they'd never met. She glanced down at the sunflower tie. Despite its amazing gaudiness, she easily recognised the expensive Italian silk in the weave. She rather liked it. In fact ...

Tania blinked rapidly, desperately willing herself to concentrate on the commission. Luke Sinclair was a prospective client. Which meant that the relationship must remain a purely professional one. By her own rigid standards, she'd already strayed beyond propriety. What on earth had prompted her subconscious in the Ferrari? Whatever it was that had tried to persuade her she was attracted to a complete stranger, definitely must *not* happen again.

'It isn't like that,' she muttered.

'Then tell me how it is.'

She cleared her throat. 'My job is to give people what they want.'

'I understood your sister to say that you not only worked to suit yourself, but that you also had an exclusive client list.'

Oh, Lord! It looked as if Ellie had, as usual, gone completely over the top.

'I do . . . work from my own agenda, that is,' Tania assured him, 'but I have to scale myself to budgets, various tastes and personal history. I slip my ideas into customer suggestions. Sometimes they take them, and sometimes they don't. I always allow space for individual style. I have to empathise with the people I work for. If they want modern for example, I give it to them — if it works.'

'And what would work here?' he asked after a fraction's pause.

Tania swung round on one heel and took in the panorama of the whole room.

'It's got to be traditional. Faded, slightly shabby elegance, a family home, dogs, children, classic paintings, chintzy chairs.' The suggestions tumbled from her lips. 'Nothing too obviously 'designed'. Just good, old-fashioned values,' she added, catching hold of his arm in her enthusiasm, and only realising what she'd done when she felt the muscles tighten under her touch.

'Sorry,' she muttered, quickly removing her hand, not noticing the flicker in Luke's eyes. 'I will do it, Luke, but I've got to do it my way — otherwise it's 'no deal'.'

'Really?' He raised his eyebrows above devastatingly blue eyes. 'I wasn't aware we'd come to an agreement yet.'

She caught her breath in her chest. How was it possible to hate Luke Sinclair so thoroughly, and in such a short space of time? She'd only known the man for about an hour, but he was stirring up emotions inside her which had lain dormant for years — making her act out of character and imagining heaven knows what between them.

If only his eyes weren't quite so blue. And his face so . . . what? He wasn't handsome. Far from it, in fact, since he had a scar which ran down the side of his nose, which looked as though it had been broken at some point. No, he wasn't particularly good looking, but there was something about him — a charisma . . . a presence which made her want to . . . to just be with him. Instinctively, she knew that they shared the same wavelength.

Of course, if she was in her right mind she shouldn't even be considering this commission, particularly as the whole set-up was totally unconventional. But then she might have blown it anyway, by telling him about her token notes. She wanted to hammer her fists in exasperation on his broad chest, make him suffer, see how he liked it. And she wished that he'd stop smiling at her. On top of everything else, she couldn't cope with it. It was as if he . . . did she know him? There was a slight flicker at the back of her mind . . . something strangely familiar about that smile of his. Perhaps they *had* met before, and that was how he knew about her work — but where? Her sister had said something about some work which she'd done for somebody. Tania would have to check when she got back to her studio, in Camden. Surely she wouldn't have forgotten someone like Luke Sinclair? There was a raw, powerful masculinity about him, which was clearly unmistakable. She was glad that she'd decided to wear her high-heeled shoes. She hated looking down, or up at clients. At a shade under six foot, her eyes were fractionally lower than his — but only just.

She squared her shoulders. Now that she was here, she might as well give it her best shot. If he turned her down flat, at least she wouldn't have given up without a fight.

'I don't normally get carried away like this,' she explained. 'But you see the fireplace, there.' She pointed across the room. 'It's crying out for a tapestry screen with peacocks in the summer, or perhaps some dried pampas grass in an old pot and a wicker basket of fir cones. And then, on winter days, roaring fires of logs cut from trees on the estate.'

She took a deep breath, almost smelling the scent of pine. 'And then, above it, we could have a Drake mirror . . . '

'Hold it!' Luke said firmly. 'We haven't talked budgets, or my requirements. I may want to turn it into a multimillion pound Business Centre.' He quite enjoyed seeing the look of horror on her face.

'You're not going to, are you?' she asked in a whispery voice which sent shivers down his spine.

He relented. 'No,' he smiled, 'I'm not. But it's a big project — Tania?' She nodded acceptance of his use of her Christian name. 'If we come to an agreement, Tania, I'd need sole use of your services. I want things done my way — quickly and professionally.'

Tania caught her breath. Was he offering her the job? It was a challenge, of course, but she could do it. She knew that she could. It would be a rash decision, too.

She didn't usually do sole projects, normally juggling several at one time. Mainly because it wasn't unknown for orders to go down the pan, businesses to fail, marriages to break up, clients to disappear without settling their accounts — or budgets agreed upon, only to be scrapped on a boardroom shake up. So if she accepted Luke's deal, she'd be totally dependent on him. It would leave her financially exposed and vulnerable. He would obviously provide references and money up front, but was she prepared to take the risk? Perhaps she was getting carried away . . . ?

A moment later she realised that there was no 'perhaps' about it. She *was* getting carried away. It was time to take a step backwards, particularly if she was going to get a firm grip on this situation.

'I don't normally . . . ' she began, then suddenly remembered Charles, her brother-in-law. Ellie had said that he was running a check on Luke Sinclair. Hadn't her sister also said that they hadn't found out much about him? Warning bells were now clanging in her brain, because Luke Sinclair didn't add up. He was English, no doubt about that, he drove an expensive car and worked in America. Which was just about the sum total of her knowledge of him. Definitely *not* a good basis for a business venture. In fact, Charles would probably go ballistic if she accepted this commission. Like Ellie, he had a habit of interfering in Tania's life. But unlike

Ellie, he was on the pompous side. More than once Tania had wanted to give him a darned good kick up the pants.

A sudden smile of devilment twisted her lips. Wasn't it Ellie who'd accused her of getting into a rut? And Ellie who'd also masterminded this whole situation? So her sister could hardly complain if Tania took her advice. Perhaps this was her chance to finally stop Ellie and Charles from trying to run her life? She should be able to manage this job with a bit of judicial juggling of assets, and if Luke Sinclair could be talked into giving her a sizeable advance . . .

Luke was searching around in his briefcase and only caught the slip-stream of her smile. His jaw tightened and Tania stopped smiling. Now what had she done? Probably not fallen in with his plans as promptly as he would have liked. Luke Sinclair was obviously a man who wanted things done his way. If they were going to work together, he was in for a shock. She liked doing things her way too! She tossed her head at him and, once again, her action made the curl of hair come tumbling down.

Luke looked up from shuffling his papers. His lips twitched and Tania had the distinct impression that he liked seeing her discomposed. She narrowed her eyes. Silent amusement was *not* her style. She was a professional, and her blood quickened at the thought of showing Luke Sinclair just how professional she could be. With a shock she realised that she hadn't felt so motivated in years.

'The builders are waiting to start. I've got landscape gardeners coming in to . . .'

'No.' Tania put a hasty hand over her mouth, but it was too late to stifle her involuntary dismay.

'I've got landscape gardeners coming in,' he continued firmly, ignoring the interruption, 'to make some sense of the mess out there.'

She couldn't let it go unchallenged.

Even if he threw her out now, she had to say something.

'Promise me . . . ' her voice wobbled, not seeming to be working properly, 'you won't . . . please no water features, or garden themes. Nothing fussy.'

'You don't like gargoyles with fountains coming out of their mouths?' His smile now took ten years off his face. 'I rather like the idea of hedges cut in the shape of peacocks.' Tania shuddered. 'Or a Japanese . . . '

'No!'

'I was about to suggest a display of garden gnomes all fishing round an ornamental pond, silver milk bottle tops on the end of their lines.'

With awful clarity, Tania realised that she'd been the victim of his particularly vile sense of humour.

'You bastard!' It was a word she rarely used, but Luke threw back his head and roared with laughter. 'What's so damned funny?' she demanded.

'Because there I was, thinking that you were a lady. Now I know better

— and it makes life a hell of a lot easier.'

Tania took a step backwards, but she wasn't quick enough to stop Luke Sinclair.

'Let me go.'

He'd grabbed her wrist and was holding it with punishing strength.

'Lighten up, Tania, and stop struggling. I'm not going to harm you. I just want your full and undivided attention for a few moments. You've done nothing but look round this room since we got here. No. Listen . . . ' He shook her wrist, not too gently. 'I was pulling your leg. I couldn't resist it and I'm sorry. But I'm serious now. The contractors will just do the heavy stuff. I'll see to everything else myself.'

'You?' Tania didn't even try to hide her scorn. He was so close to her, she could smell his maleness, a mixture of after-shave and . . . and earth? She frowned. Surely he hadn't been digging?

'Yes, me,' he said firmly.

'You wouldn't know a buddleia from a bougainvillea.'

'Now, there I may just surprise you.' From the way he spoke, Tania had no illusions on that score. She was convinced that Luke Sinclair was the type of man who could do anything, if he turned his mind to it. 'Once things get going, I intend moving back here. My work takes me all over the world, but I plan to have my base here. Just one room, tucked away on the first floor. Will that satisfy your standards of ecology?'

They were both breathing heavily now. His hold on Tania's wrist loosened as he glanced at his watch. 'I was going to suggest lunch at The Feathers, but I've got to get back to Heathrow by five.'

Tania shook her head. Food would choke her right now. He was bringing this interview from hell to a close — and not a moment too soon. Tania moved away from his body, and smoothed down her stained skirt with her hands. It helped steady them.

'Tell you what,' he continued. 'I'm due back on Friday. Make some notes — not token ones — and we'll go through them together.'

'You mean, this Friday?'

'Should be enough time. Shall we say plans, sketches or whatever, for this room and one bedroom? How about the master bedroom?'

'But I'll need access, ideas on your requirements, your . . . ' She cleared her throat. 'Your personal life.'

She took the business card from his fingers and glanced down at it — plain black lettering on stiff white card, with a string of dot.coms, email addresses and American contacts. It said a lot about the man. Even so, it wasn't enough.

'As to my personal life . . . ' Her eyes shot up to meet his. 'I shall be taking up residence here as soon as I can tie things up in the States.'

'Will your family be joining you? Your wife? Children?' She hated to sound so obvious and didn't want him to think she was snooping, but she had to know. Wives naturally had views. Their wishes needed to be included. Children too. It all made a difference.

'I shall be alone.' He snapped shut his briefcase.

'Will you be entertaining? It's a large house for a single person.'

He ignored her question. 'Do some rough sketches. We'll go from there.'

'But . . . '

'Just one thing.'

'Hmm?' Tania's attention was momentarily distracted. The sun had cut a brilliant arc of light across the lawn and, for a moment, she thought that she'd heard the mournful wail of a peacock. Her throat locked as she remembered Harry. With his golden hair, he'd looked like a young Greek god. And he'd broken her heart.

'I understand from your sister that you're not married.' The cut-glass diamond of Luke's voice scratched Tania's skin and brought her out of her reverie about Harry and lost loves.

She frowned. 'Married? No, I'm not married. I've never been married. Does it make any difference to the job?'

'Only this — and we need to get things straight from the start.'

'Get what straight?' Luke Sinclair now had her full attention.

'Your sister did a good sales job on you, although your work was already known to me.'

'Yes. I'd like to know . . . '

'She also seemed at pains to stress your marital status.'

Tania's cheeks flamed in embarrassment. One day she really would murder Ellie, she promised herself grimly. Family loyalty prevented her from explaining Ellie's mission in life, but only just.

She was toying with several plausible explanations, when Luke said, 'I'm not married, either, but neither am I looking for a wife. So any ambitions you may have had in that direction — particularly regarding this job

— must be firmly quashed.'

Tania's cheeks were stinging from the verbal slap, which he'd just inflicted on her.

The arrogance of the man! Did he seriously think that she was in the least bit interested in him? She'd rather die than get involved with a dinosaur, who thought that a woman's only aim in life was to grab a man.

More than ever grateful for her Italian high-heeled shoes, she flung her head back. She didn't have to look up at him. She was so angry, her height must have risen the necessary two inches for her to eyeball him.

'Since you are clearly reluctant to give me your personal details, I'll give you mine. I have never been married. I am not interested in getting married. I have no children, but I am not a virgin. I am not sexually frustrated. I have looked after myself since the age of eighteen, without help from anyone.

'You may think you're God's gift to women,' Mr Sinclair,' she continued icily. 'But as far as I'm concerned, you're just another over-opinionated male, with an inflated ego — who seems to think that a single woman of my age can't wait to drag him into a relationship. Well, I'm sorry to disappoint you.' She snatched up her briefcase. 'I hope you find a suitably married person to take on your work. Whoever it is, he or she has my deepest sympathy!'

She wished that wretched curl wouldn't keep bobbing about as she spoke. It was a serious distraction, and she could see by the light of amusement in Luke's eyes that he was finding it rather comical too. She wanted to slap the smile right off his face. Unfortunately, Luke Sinclair looked the sort of man who might very well slap her back.

Very slowly, he held out a pair of house keys. 'Much as I hate to cut short this riveting exchange of views, healthy though it is, I really do have to get back to Heathrow. Here, let yourself in with these. I should be back by the end of the week and we'll talk again then. Would you like to freshen up, attend to your hair perhaps, before I drive you back to The Feathers?'

As if letting out its own sigh of relief, all her hair finally escaped its neat pleat and, in the best tradition of a movie cliché, it quickly tumbled down around her shoulders. Tania had never felt so humiliated in her life.

Luke raised a hand as if to touch it, then with a gentle smile of regret, he said, 'I'll run you back to the village. You can freshen up there.'

3

Tania's telephone was ringing as she unlocked her front door.

'How did you get on?'

'Hi Ellie.' Tania shrugged herself out of her jacket. She was desperately tired and dying for a bath.

'Well?'

Tania couldn't resist a tantalising smile. Ellie was practically squeaking with curiosity. She decided to let Ellie squeak a little longer. It was nice to have the upper hand in a conversation with her sister — and a novelty.

'How are you, Ellie? Did you have a good weekend? I tried phoning you, but . . . '

'Tania!' her sister howled down the line.

'Yes?'

'Luke Sinclair.'

'What about him?'

'Are you being infuriating on purpose?'

Tania was, but she wasn't going to admit it. She glanced down the corridor. Her neat bathroom beckoned. There was also Friday night's unfinished bottle of Chardonnay cooling in the fridge.

'Look Ellie, I've only just got back.'

'I know. I've been trying to get you for hours.'

Tania glanced down at the answering machine. Several messages blinked. She stretched the back of her neck. What she would have killed for was a luxurious bath, a light supper, and that video which she still hadn't got around to watching.

Some hope! a small voice grumbled inside her head. No chance of an early night. She'd have to make an immediate start on her sketches and ideas. Which involved making some telephone calls and finishing up the work in hand. Then The Peacock House was all hers. She felt a small tremor of excitement in the pit of her stomach.

'Sorry Ellie. I can't talk now.'

'What?'

'I've got work to do.'

'Well, really!' her sister huffed. 'Is this any way to treat me? I set the whole thing up, remember?'

'Against my wishes,' Tania reminded her pointedly.

Ellie ignored that one. 'And what about Charles?'

'That reminds me, Ellie. Has Charles found out anything about Luke Sinclair?'

'What if he has?' It was Ellie's turn to be difficult. Tania could imagine her tossing her blonde head. She obviously wasn't going to let Tania off the hook lightly — not until some serious grovelling had taken place.

'I need to know, please.' Desperate needs dictated desperate measures, Tania told herself, hoping that Ellie wouldn't keep her dangling too long.

'Why?'

'I'm thinking of doing the work.' She

waited for the fireworks.

'I knew it!' Tania held the receiver away from her ear as Ellie exploded with delight down the other end. 'You were absolutely right for the job. Wait till I tell Charles. That's fantastic.' She babbled on with loads of other questions about Luke, but Tania didn't answer any of them. She wasn't sure that she had the answers anyway. Ellie eventually ground to a halt as she ran out of things to say.

'What has Charles got on Luke Sinclair?' Tania was finally able to ask again.

There was a small pause before her sister said, with a tad less exuberance than usual, 'Actually Charles is being a bit stinky about the whole thing. He won't tell me.'

'Can't or won't?'

'Can't, more likely, although he hasn't said as much. It looks like this Luke Sinclair guards his privacy pretty carefully.'

Tell me about it, thought Tania.

As Ellie clearly didn't have any news to impart, Tania didn't see any point in prolonging the conversation. Ellie was clearly miffed as Tania cut short the call, but Tania didn't have time for her little sister's finer feelings. She had work to do.

★　★　★

Two nights later, after practically working non-stop for forty-eight hours, Tania dragged herself to bed and was asleep, almost before her head had touched the pillow. What seemed only a second later, the alarm jangled into life and she rolled over with a groan. She'd always had trouble waking up in the morning and had bought herself a high-volume alarm clock. This morning, it appeared to be doing a more than efficient job.

Opening her eyes to chuck it over on to a chair, she realised that she must have made a mistake when setting the alarm.

'Five o'clock . . . ?' she moaned. It was supposed to be set it for eight. 'Shut up, damn you!' She was shaking it when she heard her recording machine cut in as the ringing stopped.

'Tania — are you there?' A male voice demanded.

Tania fought the sheets as she tried to snatch up the telephone. It had to be an emergency for someone to ring at this unearthly hour.

'Hello? Charles? I was asleep. What's wrong? Is it Ellie? The boys?'

'Tania . . . ?' She stiffened. The voice didn't sound like Charles — it sounded suspiciously like Luke Sinclair.

'Tania?' It *was* Luke!

Anger bit in. 'Have you gone mad?' Tania exploded. 'Are you aware what time it is?'

'Look, I know. I'm sorry. And you're not going to like what I'm about to say.'

Tania felt sick in the pit of her stomach. The deal must have fallen through. Why else would Luke Sinclair be on the phone at this time of the morning? She clenched her jaw and prepared to bite the bullet. She'd never been any good at the revenge thing. But right now, she felt angry with the whole world.

'The contractor's just been on the telephone to me . . .'

Tania wasn't listening. She'd been a fool to cancel her other work. Perhaps it wasn't too late to get some of it back? Why on earth had she let petty prejudices influence her basic business principles? She should *never* have taken Luke Sinclair on as a sole client. It had been a silly scheme to try get even with Ellie — and Charles. It just showed she wasn't cut out for that sort of thing.

' . . . There's been a break in.'

'I see. Thanks for letting me know. It could have waited.' She didn't know whether to be thankful or annoyed. At least he hadn't let her waste her time on the project, but five o'clock in the morning calls were definitely not her favourite form of communication.

'You've got the keys.'

'What? Oh yes, I have. In my bag. I'll get them back to you. Is there an agent or someone I can leave them with?'

'I'm sorry . . . ? The line's not very clear. I can't get away right now and I . . . well, I know that it's a cheek and you've every right to refuse, but do you think you could go down there? Check it out for me?'

'Check out what . . . ?'

'The damage. I don't think it's serious — just a bit of vandalism. But now that we're going ahead with the project, I don't want to waste time clearing up after the local yobs have broken every window in the place, or evicting squatters. Don't do anything heroic. If it looks like trouble, then just call the police.'

Tania's feet slipped on the sheets as she struggled to sit up straight. She never closed her curtains at night, and streaks of dawn were painting the grey sky a delicate shade or pearl pink. Just for a moment, she let herself look at it. When she was awake at this hour, she loved this time of day. It was quiet and full of hope. The lock was peaceful and she regularly sat out on her tiny balcony, enjoying the early morning water noises. She'd often seen the sun rise when she and Harry had been an item. She gave a little sigh, a mixture of nostalgia and drowned hopes.

'How soon do you think you can get down there?'

'Where?' she asked dreamily, not paying attention to what Luke was saying.

'Are you listening Tania?' Luke raised his voice. 'Little Chipping, of course. Where d'you think I mean? Look, I'm sorry if you're in bed. Or if you've got someone with you.' Even across the Atlantic, the sarcasm in his voice was unmistakable.

'How dare you?' She was paying full attention now. 'I don't appreciate being woken up in the middle of the night to have personal comments made about my love life.' She didn't add — 'or lack of it'. That was something which Luke

Sinclair didn't need to know.

His words cut in again just as she was about to slam down the receiver.

'That was out of order.' Tania noticed that he didn't apologise. 'Can you do this for me? Can you go down to Little Chipping?'

'Everything's off, isn't it?'

'Tania, can we save this for another time? It's very much 'on' — and I need your help. Please. You're not backing out are you?'

There was no mistaking the urgency in his voice. It was at times like this, that Tania wished she still smoked. There was none of the brash executive about Luke Sinclair now. He needed help . . . and he'd turned to her. She felt a warm flush gurgling around in her stomach.

'No. I'm still up for it.'

'When can you get there?

'This afternoon?' To her horror, she found herself offering the impossible.

'Great, Tania. I owe you one.'

Tania was still coming to terms with

what she'd done, when she heard an unmistakable female voice, presumably in Luke's bedroom, complaining, 'Luke, hurry up. I'm waiting!'

Tania's warm flush went cold.

'Better go. Got a meeting.'

I'll bet! Tania thought grimly as she replaced the receiver very carefully, having no problem in guessing the *exact* nature of Luke's meeting. The whole thing smacked of 'Good Old Tania — she'll sort out my problems'. Unlike herself, his in-house female companion clearly wouldn't allow herself to be dragged out of bed at sparrow spit, to go haring down to Little Chipping on some wild goose chase.

Tania yawned and stretched. There wasn't time to think about the females in Luke Sinclair's life. He was obviously a virile man, who was likely to attract women by the score. Technically, he might be single, but in practice Tania doubted that he was on his own very often . . . if at all. Just why she found that thought depressing, she wasn't sure. Luke Sinclair's personal life was none of her business. He'd made that absolutely clear. What wasn't quite so clear, was why he had actually offered her the job — particularly when he appeared to be so against unattached females.

She pushed the sheets aside. Officially, she wasn't sure whether she still had the job, but he had asked for her help. If she worked at double speed, she should *just* get to Little Chipping by late afternoon. She smiled ruefully. Was it only a week ago, that Ellie had been accusing her of being stuck in a rut? Tania headed towards the kitchen. Before she did anything, she was going to make herself a gallon of black coffee!

★ ★ ★

'I've mended the window and put new locks on the doors, Miss Jordan. Here are the keys. Apart from that, there doesn't seem to be too much damage. Probably just local kids.'

'Have you been round the rest of the house?'

'Yes. But like I explained to the guv'nor, I don't want the responsibility of looking after the house in his absence. I'm prepared to arrange night security, but I can't do anything today. It's too late. What do you think?'

Tania wasn't exactly sure what she thought, or how much responsibility Luke had given her.

'Have you tried contacting Mr Sinclair?'

'I telephoned him in the States. He said that he was sending his representative down. That's you, isn't it?'

Tania supposed it was. The builder seemed to have made a good job of repairing the damage which, at first glance, looked to be fairly superficial. The house itself hadn't been vandalised, apart from the window, and a quick check on the premises had shown there were no squatters.

'Is the house safe?'

'Don't get you?'

'I meant — is it secure?'

'Well, now . . . ' The builder clearly wasn't about to commit himself. 'Like I said, I don't want . . . '

Tania cut the man short. 'If I stay tonight, can you get a proper guard here, for tomorrow?'

'If that's what Mr Sinclair wants,' the builder said reluctantly.

'I'll speak to him,' Tania said, 'if you make all the arrangements.'

She watched the builder drive off in his van. The evening air fanned her face and she decided to take a walk in the gardens. This time, she'd come prepared — sleeping bag, hot water bottle, pyjamas, Wellington boots, thick sweaters and jeans. No business suits to stain or high heels to sink in the mud, and her hair was simply tied back, with just a few escaping tendrils softening her face.

She locked the door carefully behind her, pocketing the new key, and smiling with the pure joy of the evening. She hadn't slept much over the last sixty hours — and yet, she'd never felt more alive in her life. The garden was a riot of nature, with the birds singing to each other from every available perch. The prunus was an explosion of pink blossoms, with just a few fallen petals swaying on the rising blades of grass.

She picked her way down what had once been steps to the rockery. The ground was wet and slippery, and she moved carefully. Luke was right — it *was* a mess. The grass was a mini-jungle and she couldn't even make out where the tennis court had been. The wall to the kitchen garden was a pile of rubble. She remembered the time when she was a child, and how Mr Harrison, the gardener, would let her shell peas and eat them fresh from the pod. He'd once caught her stealing gooseberries and had pretended not to notice. He'd been a kind man. In fact, it seemed as if everyone had been nice to her in those days. Perhaps that's why she had such happy memories of the house . . . ?

She perched on the safest bit of

rubble and looked back at the house. It seemed to be smiling at her as if it also remembered those happy times. Tania's vision blurred. If she did her best by it she hoped that Luke would treat it well.

Of course, it was stupid to feel sentimental about a house which she hadn't even lived in, but the Fitzroys had been very generous to their cleaning woman's eldest daughter, welcoming her to all their winter and summer parties — until she'd committed the unforgivable sin of falling in love with their only son. Then the class divide had reared its ugly head and she'd no longer been so welcome. They hadn't turned her away, or been openly rude. However, invitations were no longer automatically issued, and Harry had found himself unexpectedly paired-up for family dinner parties, with the suitable daughter of a business acquaintance of his father, or an old friend of his mother's. It was ironic, really, that it was Patti who'd been in the car with him when he'd died.

Tania's mother, who was just as keen on the social order of things, would have placed Patti as far below them, using the same scale, as the Fitzroys had placed her own daughter.

Tania stood up. A lot of water from the River Leach had passed under the little bridge since those days. Social divides were a thing of the past. There was no one left to care any more. She doubted if anyone even remembered. Harry's accident had been a scandal at the time — rumours of a night race with a motorbike, which had driven him off the road and promptly disappeared, had been rife — but time had passed and gradually everyone had forgotten. Tania thought that she had also forgotten, until last week.

She shivered. The night air was growing chilly, and her feet were getting cold despite her thick socks and boots.

Over a mug of soup and a smelly paraffin heater, Tania tried calling Luke's numbers on her mobile. However, there was no reply from any of them. The nearest she got was a recording, but as the female voice sounded suspiciously like the one which she'd heard in his bedroom that morning, she didn't leave a message.

She went over her drawings again, pleased with her work. She felt like Cinderella invited to the ball. It was a chance in a million to do up the house — a dream come true.

After that, there was nothing else she could do. Her eyes began to feel heavy and she decided to unroll her sleeping bag in the master bedroom. She also laid out a few swatches of material. It was important to know how the different times of day worked on them. A particular piece could look wonderful in the morning and hideous by sunset. Tania stepped back. Even with the gloomy basic lighting the builders had rigged up, the green velvet seemed to work. Her fingertips tingled. She'd had that special feeling which she always got when she knew that she was on to a winner. She hoped Luke Sinclair would feel the same way.

Smiling, Tania shook out a very unflattering pair of winceyette pyjamas, decorated with pink elephants. She'd brought them years ago, when she'd had a bout of flu and couldn't stop shivering. They'd only been worn once. And looking at them now, she could understand why. They were enormous, unflattering, passion-killers.

Tania put them on with a pair of bed socks, grabbed her hot water bottle and dived into her sleeping bag. It was bliss. She didn't remember falling asleep.

It was dark when she woke up. It took her a moment or two to gather her wits, before she remembered where she was and felt able to relax. It was very quiet outside, and all the wildlife out in the garden had clearly bedded down for the night. what then had woken her?

A moment later heard a loud sound coming from downstairs. Groping for her torch, she snapped it on. Illuminating the room with its powerful beam. Heart thumping, she struggled out of

74

her sleeping bag, straining her ears for the sound of more noise.

Padding round the room, she decided not to bother with slippers — besides, they probably wouldn't fit over her enormous bed socks. Better to surprise her intruder. Hoping it wasn't a badger or a vagrant, she crept out of the bedroom, wondering if the local yobs had returned? She began to realise it had been foolish to stay here on her own. Especially since she was likely to be no match for a gang of troublemakers. Her body tightened at the thought. But she wasn't scared — just furiously angry. In fact, if she caught anyone trying to damage the property, she was fully prepared to give as good as she got.

She could hear her fractured breathing in the quiet of the night as she leaned over the banister. She couldn't see any foreign shapes in the half-light, either animal or human. There was no one there. Nights in the heart of the country were always full of funny noises, she recalled with a sigh of relief. Just as she was turning back to her makeshift bedroom, there was a very loud crash of breaking glass. Tania's feet froze to the floor, no doubt in her mind now. Wildlife didn't break windows on that scale. The intruders were back!

She scuttled into her room. Her mobile. Where was it? Too late, she remembered that she'd left it in the kitchen when she'd been having her supper and going through her paper-work.

Think straight! she thought franti-cally. Don't lose it! You've got to get help. Perhaps it wasn't the kitchen window they broke?

She'd have to chance it. Turning off her torch she decided to take it downstairs with her. It was long and black and might prove a useful weapon. She gave a couple of experimental swings on the landing and, deciding it could do the job with honours if she was attacked, she began to creep slowly down the stairs which creaked ominously under her weight.

Tania stiffened, holding her breath for a few moments before continuing her slow progress. Halfway down her courage deserted her. This was mindless! What if there were several of them? She didn't stand a hope — one woman in elephant pyjamas with only a torch for protection!

She turned to run back up to her room and tripped over the bobble of her bed socks. Her knees hit the edge of the stair with a crack. She clutched at the ledge and bit down a sob of pain. There was nothing else for it. She *had* to get to her phone. She swivelled round on her winceyette-covered bottom, amazed that she hadn't made enough noise to alert a hoard of burglars. Then, clutching the banister rail, she inched on down the stairs.

Easing open the kitchen door, she was hit by a cold blast of night air coming from the broken windowpane. She stifled a shriek. *A black silhouette was climbing through the window!*

Not giving herself time to think, she whirled her torch and with a Ninja cry, cracked it down heavily on the intruder's head. With an oath that made her hair stand on end, the intruder fell to the floor.

Not caring if the intruder was dead, she slid across the room in her sock-clad feet intent on snatching up her mobile. There was a noise of moving body behind her. The intruder wasn't dead. The intruder beat her to it.

'Give it to me,' she screamed. 'I'm armed.'

'Let go of the torch!'

'I'll hit you again if you don't let me have it.'

'I've already got a lump the size of an ostrich egg behind my ear. What on earth are you playing at?'

'You needn't think I'm alone. I'll call out. Mr Sinclair's upstairs and the police are coming.'

'The police may be coming, but Mr Sinclair sure as hell isn't upstairs.'

'Yes, he is.'

'Mr Sinclair's down here.'

'W . . . what?' Tania's mouth fell open as the intruder flicked a switch. The kitchen was instantly bathed in light.

For the second morning running, Tania had been woken up at five o'clock by Luke Sinclair!

4

'What on earth are you wearing?'

Luke's blue eyes raked Tania's body — from the bobbles on her woollen bed socks, up over her pink elephant pyjamas, to the tendrils of hair fanning her face.

Tania let out a steam engine hiss of breath. 'What on earth does it matter what I'm wearing?'

Luke took a step forwards, and instinctively Tania took one backwards. Her heartbeat still hadn't recovered from the shock of discovering Luke Sinclair clambering through the window, and she was well aware of only being clad in her pyjamas — a fact which obviously hadn't escaped Luke's attention!

'You look like an extra elephant, who's just escaped from the circus.' The corners of his mouth curved and he took another step forward.

'What are you doing here?' Tania snapped, a furnace slowly building up inside her. How *dare* Luke Sinclair scare the living daylights out of her, by breaking in like a burglar? He'd got her up here under false pretences. To the best of her memory he was supposed to be in the United States.

'It's my house. Remember?'

'Then why don't you come through the door like a normal person, instead of breaking in through the window? Or is that your usual method of entry?' she added sarcastically.

'Because someone's changed the locks and my keys don't fit.' He spoke patiently as if addressing a small child.

'You could have rung the bell.' Tania was getting hotter by the second. It was unnerving being semi-clad and alone with Luke — especially after midnight.

'Look, do you mind if I sit down?' Luke sagged against the table. 'That was quite a thump you gave me.'

Tania shifted her socked feet uncomfortably. He did look pale, she thought guiltily, as he collapsed on to a kitchen chair. She'd put a lot of muscle into her swing.

'I'm sorry . . . ' they both began and stopped.

Luke smiled. 'You first. It hurts a bit to talk. I'll just sit and rub my bump while you apologise.'

'Well . . . I didn't mean to hit you quite so hard.'

'Apology accepted.' The colour began to return to Luke's face. 'And I'm sorry I didn't enter by more conventional means.' Tania didn't think she'd seen anything so pulse-racing as the slow smile which moved his lips. 'There, that's the formalities over with.'

Tania cleared her throat as her heart sort of trip-switched out.

'How's your bump now?' she managed to ask.

Tania watched Luke rub it experimentally, a frown creasing his forehead.

It really did look as if she'd hit him far too enthusiastically.

'I'll live. In training for the New York cops, are we? I understand they carry lethal weapons like that thing. What is it, by the way? The spinster's fail-safe attack kit?'

'It's my torch.' Tania told him curtly, her sympathy swiftly evaporating. 'Do you have a problem with my marital status?'

'Very efficient piece of equipment.' Luke ignored her question. His eyes seemed to be fixed on her pyjama jacket. 'That, and your choice of nightwear, must do an excellent job in discouraging unwelcome attention.'

Suddenly aware that the top buttons of her pyjamas had worked themselves loose, Tania drew the gaping jacket round the top half of her body and wished that she'd worn her dressing gown — although Luke Sinclair would probably have unflattering views of flowery candlewick. She was aware of Luke's eyes following her fingers as they fumbled for buttons and button-holes. It wasn't easy doing them up with ten thumbs, but that was how her fingers felt at the moment.

Looking up, she found herself being treated once again to Luke's lazy smile — and once again Tania felt her insides turning to liquid.

'You're supposed to be in America,' she told him sternly. 'Not creeping round the English countryside in the dark, frightening the wits out of the locals.'

Tania knew that she was being irrational, but Luke Sinclair was stirring her hormones every which way, which had the result of making her act totally out of character. Ellie wouldn't believe it if she could see her super-cool sister now: pyjama clad, after clouting Luke Sinclair over the head with her torch.

'Meeting was cancelled. Got an early flight. I drove straight up here from Heathrow.' He was still rubbing his head. 'That was quite a reception.'

Through the broken windowpane,

Tania could hear alarming garden noises. However, with Luke sitting at the table — admittedly a bit pale, but physically present — she felt secure. For almost the first time, she realised just how isolated The Peacock House was. Before tonight, she'd never been alone here. There'd always been lots of people around. She shivered.

'You are alone I take it?' Luke asked his eyes picking up her involuntary movement.

'Yes.'

'At the risk of sounding ungrateful, you do realise it was a really stupid thing to do — staying here all on your own with only a mobile and a torch for protection? Anything could have happened to you.'

'Well, it didn't.' Tania tossed her head back. 'And whatever happened to 'thank you'? It may have escaped your attention, but I'm only here because of you! So, if anything had happened to me, it would have been all your fault.'

She hadn't meant to sound so sharp, but Luke was serious dynamite on legs. She'd never felt like this about any other man — even Harry — and she was severely out of practice with the emotions bubbling around her body. They were also highly dangerous. Hadn't Luke Sinclair made his feelings on their professional status more than clear? No involvement.

The corners of his eyes creased in evident enjoyment. Tania clenched her hands to stop them shaking. The loathsome creature was actually enjoying the situation. Tania went from hot to cold, desperately praying that he couldn't read her thoughts. She was never any good with body language either, and could only hope that he couldn't read that too.

'Thank you,' he said with a brief nod, his expression now inscrutable. 'And I can only put my lack of manners down to that crack on the head. I've still got double vision. You pack a powerful whack.'

'And I can look after myself in any situation.'

The appreciative smile was back again. 'Yes, I can see that. You're — ah — very healthy.'

Tania swallowed, wondering what on earth to say next. Luke took the decision out of her hands.

'Even so — promise me you won't stay here alone again?' His voice was gentle and for a moment Tania was fooled into thinking he cared. Until he ruined it by adding, 'I'm not covered by insurance.'

She took a deep breath, but Luke beat her to it again. 'I thought you'd have had the sense to stay at The Feathers. You won't take another swipe at me if I ask why you're here?'

'The builder said he'd fix up some security, but he couldn't arrange anything until tomorrow. I didn't want to leave the house empty, not after what happened last night.' Her teeth began to chatter from cold, delayed shock, and the other sensations in her limbs which she was still too scared to identify.

Assessing the situation in an instant, Luke rummaged in the holdall, which he'd dropped on the floor when Tania's torch had come into contact with his skull. He dragged out some whisky and poured a generous shot into a mug. 'Drink this.'

Tania shook her head. 'I don't . . . '

'Drink it!' He thrust the mug into her hands. 'Or do you want me to personally pour it down your throat?'

'Put like that,' she gritted her teeth, 'how could I refuse?'

'That's my girl,' he said grimly.

By now Tania's hands were shaking so badly that she could hardly raise the mug to her lips. Considering the knock he'd just taken, Luke was out of his chair with surprising speed. Putting his hand round hers, he gently lifted the rim of the mug to her lips. He was so close to Tania that she could have raised a hand to stroke the stubble on his chin. She wanted to . . . badly. To her horror, she felt the firm contours of his body against hers as she leaned towards him for support.

'Better?' His voice set her body on fire, like the burning liquid which he'd forced her to swallow.

'Yes.' Her reply was an unattractive hoarse croak. She blinked down the tears in her eyes, for the first time appreciating why it was called firewater.

Luke tucked a curl of hair, which she'd just dunked in her whisky, firmly behind her ear. Releasing her very gently, he poured himself some whisky and sat back down again opposite her.

'You should always wear your hair loose,' he said. 'It makes you look less like a school teacher.'

Tania couldn't stop blinking. It must be the drink, she thought, as Luke's face swam in and out of focus. He had no right to look so gorgeous — especially after a long transatlantic flight. In his black leather jacket and jeans, he was to die for.

Tania raised fingers to her hair scrunch, which was doing a very poor job. Luke put out a hand, anchoring her wrist to the table.

'Leave it.'

'You just said . . . '

'I said I liked your hair like that. You should wear it loose all the time. In fact,' he lowered his voice forcing Tania to lean forward, 'I might just insist that you do so, while you're staying here.'

Tania jerked away from Luke as though she'd been stung. 'May I remind you that our relationship is a purely professional one? Your words — not mine.' She struggled. 'Let me go!'

'The question now is . . . ' he murmured, not letting go of her wrist, ' . . . what are we going to do with the rest of the night? Or should I say, early morning?'

'Do? Nothing, of course!'

'Nothing?'

Tania closed her eyes. She didn't have a clue what Luke was talking about. First thing in the morning, she was going back to Camden. She'd definitely made up her mind. There were forces at work here which she couldn't fight.

'Tania?' He shook her wrist. 'You haven't gone to sleep on me, have you?'

'What is there to do?' she forced herself to ask as she opened her eyes. The expression in Luke's was making her feel dizzy.

He finally let go of her wrist, stretched and stifled a yawn. 'I don't know what you have in mind, but I need some sleep.' He ran a hand through his dark hair, causing it to stand up on end. He looked like a little boy who'd just woken up. 'Any objection?'

'Sleep?'

'Yes. Sleep. Now what have I said to turn your eyes that interesting shade of cobalt?'

'Nothing. Of course you can go to sleep.'

'Good.' Luke swung the holdall up over his shoulder. 'See you in the morning then.'

Before Tania quite realised it, he'd sauntered out of the room and up the stairs.

'Where're you going?' she called after him, but there was no response.

Grabbing her torch and mobile phone, she turned out the kitchen light and raced up the stairs in the dark, cannoning into Luke as he came to a halt in the doorway of the master bedroom.

His eyes swept over the swatches of cloth, her radio, bedside lamp, discarded hot water bottle, empty mug of cocoa and sleeping bag.

'I see you've made yourself at home.'

'I didn't know you'd be back. I . . . '

As Luke turned around to face her, their bodies collided. With the shock of the impact — she could have sworn that Luke's lips had, in the darkness, briefly grazed her forehead — Tania dropped her torch. He swore softly, although she wasn't sure if it was because her torch had landed on his toes, or because of their collision.

Temporarily unable to think straight, she let her head rest gently against the firm wall of his chest. It felt safe and solid.

He released her very gently. 'I'll shake down in the study. Sleep well.'

Tania stayed where she was for a few moments, listening to Luke's footsteps on the bare floorboards. She wasn't sure that she could move without falling over, and she didn't want Luke coming back down the corridor to pick her up. Her flesh would go into open rebellion.

★   ★   ★

The sun cut a brilliant swathe through the window and the birds were in full voice as Tania blinked awake. She'd obviously slept like the dead. Even her high volume alarm hadn't woken her, and it was gone ten o'clock. Her eyes felt clogged with grit and her tongue parched and dry as she remembered with disgust last night's — or should it be this morning's? — slug of whisky. She scrambled out of her sleeping bag and ripped off her pyjamas, vowing never to wear the dreadful things again, as they fell in a pink crumpled heap on to the floor. Luke was quite right. They were horrible!

With the briefest of washes in the hand basin and a quick comb of her hair, Tania was ready. As she opened the door, an enticing smell of bacon and toast met her nostrils. Her stomach gave an unattractive grumble, angrily reminding her it had only had a meagre bowl of soup the night before.

'Ah, there you are. Did you sleep well?'

Luke, looking none the worse for his nocturnal adventure, was wearing a white sweatshirt and jeans. He moved easily round the kitchen as if he were used to catering for himself.

'Yes. Thank you.'

'Sit down and help yourself to coffee. Luckily the village shop was open. Breakfast won't be long. One egg or two?' 'Two, I think,' he said, looking up from the frying pan with his devastating smile. Tania watched the egg frying next to the sizzling bacon, her mouth watering in anticipation.

'There's some toast if you can't wait,' Luke added, nodding towards the table before turning his attention back to the frying pan.

Tania quickly buttered a slice of toast. Her bowl of soup was about the only thing she remembered eating the day before, and she'd always had a healthy appetite.

'You're very self-sufficient.'

'Comes of living alone,' Luke said, serving up two generous plates of eggs and bacon. 'Don't let it get cold.' He tossed the pan into a dish of soapy water and sat down. 'Glad to see that you followed my advice.'

Tania poised, her fork halfway to her mouth. 'Advice?'

'Your hair.'

Tania didn't need to look in the mirror to know that she was doing an excellent impersonation of a ripe tomato.

Having overslept, and in a hurry to get dressed this morning, she'd just shoved a couple of hairpins in the back of her hair — something which she often did when she was working from home. It wasn't elegant, but it did at least keep her hair out of her eyes. Only now, when it was too late, she remembered what Luke had said last night about her hair. The wretch was grinning at her now, obviously under the false impression that she'd done it for his benefit.

'I dressed in a hurry,' she said as loftily as she could manage.

'So I see. The casual look suits you.'

Tania glanced down at her shirt just to make sure the necessary number of shirt buttons were done up. She'd already decided that she was going to leave after breakfast. Now Luke was here, he could sort out his own security arrangements. But she wasn't missing another meal. Her system would go on strike if she did.

'So . . . ' Luke waved a fork at her. 'You're thinking of green velvet for the bedroom? Saw a bit of it draped over a chair last night,' he explained.

'Mmm, yes I do,' Tania muttered through a mouthful of toast. 'It's a very ecological colour and works well in most rooms. I thought a paler green for the carpets and green velvet curtains. It should go well with any other décor you had in mind.'

'Go on.' Luke poured them both some more coffee. He was instantly businesslike.

'It depends on your personal taste, but I thinking of a minimalist approach to furnishings in the upstairs room.'

'And downstairs?'

Tania put down her knife and fork. 'Ivory silk wallpaper in the drawing room, cool and uncluttered. Lots of coloured throws on the floor: multi-coloured, for dogs, children or whatever. In the summer, the French windows should open out on to the patio, filled with tubs of bright flowers, and there'd also be space for a barbecue. There's an old tennis court in the garden, which clearly needs attention, and . . . '

'You obviously see this as a family house?'

Tania pushed her plate away, her appetite deserting her. They were back to the subject of marriage! She took a deep breath. As she didn't intend staying here any longer than she had to, Tania supposed it didn't really matter what she said.

'You told me that you intended to live here alone. However, I also had to consider the possibility that you might eventually have a wife and family.' She ran a nervous hand through her hair. 'But it's proving impossible for me to work with you. Because, every time I make a comment about your personal situation, you immediately assume that I have an ulterior motive. Which of course I don't. But to do my job properly, I have to know your personal circumstances. So, you can believe what you like — but I am *not* angling for a husband!'

Jumping to her feet, she pushed her chair back with such force that it crashed to the floor behind her. Flummoxed and embarrassed, she quickly bent down to pick it up. She disliked scenes. They made her feel hot and uncomfortable and she wasn't good at handling them.

Luke rose slowly to his feet..

'When you're angry,' he said softly, 'the tip of your nose goes bright pink.'

'I'm *not* angry,' Tania retorted furiously. 'It's just . . . ' She gave a heavy sigh, before raising her hands in a gesture of resignation. 'As you know, this commission wasn't my idea. It was fixed up between you and my sister, Ellie, who's forever trying . . . ' Tania hesitated for a moment, and then decided to go for broke. 'To tell the truth, Ellie is forever trying to get me married off, and seems to think that finding me work is one way of achieving her aim. Which is very stupid of her. So I'm sorry that I've wasted your time. I'll pack up my bits and pieces and leave.'

'This house is special for you, isn't it?' Luke's voice was doing its gentle bit again. Tania wished he wouldn't. It destroyed her concentration. 'You've been here before, haven't you?' he added quietly.

'I don't want to talk about it,' she muttered.

'I take it that's a yes?' Tania hesitated then gave a brief nod. 'Why don't you want to discuss it?'

'It was a long time ago.'

'Does the memory hurt so much?'

Tania blinked hard. She really wished Luke wouldn't talk as if he cared.

He'd opened the door fully to get the benefit of the morning sun. Tania smiled, unaware of how her expression changed her face. Luke breathed in sharply as he watched her struggle with her explanation, her eyes both dreamy and melancholy at the same time.

'The peacocks used to come to that

door to get kitchen scraps. There was one very bold one who used to wail piteously until it was fed. He was extremely greedy. There was a gardener here, Mr Harrison. He used to feed it too.'

'Was it this gardener who made you unhappy?'

'Oh no, I liked him. He was kind to me. I loved the house and gardens too.' She paused. 'You may as well know . . . I was unofficially engaged to Harry Fitzroy. His parents owned this house.'

'I see.'

Now she'd started, Tania couldn't seem to stop herself. She didn't notice how Luke's voice had hardened or how stiff and rigid he'd become.

'My mother was the cleaning lady here,' she told him. 'Harry's parents wouldn't have approved of the match and neither would my mother, which is why we kept quiet about it. We were young and I suppose we thought they would change their minds. Ellie's younger than me. She knew nothing about the relationship. She just knew I was very happy here. Then, one night there was a terrible accident. The official explanation was that one of the peacocks had strolled into the path of Harry's car; that he'd swerved to avoid it and hit a tree.'

'You don't believe it?'

'It's possible. He always drove very fast.'

'But . . . ?'

'Patti Saunders was in the car with him — and he'd been drinking.'

'I don't see the connection.'

'We were supposed to meet up that night in Stow-in-the-Wold. Harry's parents were away . . . ' Tania cleared her throat, carefully not meeting Luke's eyes. 'We . . . we hadn't seen each other for ages. We thought we'd make a night of it. Harry's parents had done their best to keep us apart. So had my mother. I was late because my mother wasn't well. I think she suspected I had a date with Harry and tried to keep me in. Harry didn't like being kept waiting so, by the time I got to the pub, he'd gone. The barman told me he'd had several drinks with a gang of bikers who used to hang out locally, and then gone off with Patti Saunders, the barmaid. I never saw him again. I think he was showing off. The car was a powerful one and, as I said, he drove it far too fast. It was an accident, but I don't think the peacock caused it.'

'What do you think happened?'

The pain was so physical now Tania wanted to cry out loud. 'There was a rumour ... a race with one of the bikers ... skid marks on the grass verge. I don't know ... I sort of blanked it all out.'

Luke walked slowly towards her and placed his arms on her shoulders, forcing her to look up at him.

'It's time to let go of the past, Tania.'

'I thought I had until I came back, but it's still there.'

'Do you still want the job?'

Tania swallowed. 'More than anything in the world.'

'Then it's yours. Now, let's think about the future.' Luke raised a thumb to her face and stroked her cheek. Until then, Tania hadn't realised that there'd been tears in her eyes.

He moved his face closer to hers and she suddenly realised that there was something disturbingly familiar about Luke Sinclair . . . Tania blinked as a shutter seemed to open briefly, before crashing down again on her memory. She *had* seen him before! But where? She tensed her neck muscles. Luke's face was now far too close to hers for her sanity.

'The future . . . ?' she muttered helplessly.

'This house. Our relationship.'

'We don't have one.'

'Professionally we do,' he drawled. 'Or were you . . . '

'Stop it. Stop putting words into my mouth.'

'Spikes down. I'm only teasing.'

'Then you've got a very warped sense of humour.'

'I'm not sure you should be speaking to your employer in such disrespectful terms!'

'Go ahead and dismiss me then.' Tania raised her clenched jaw, pleased to note that her eyes were almost on the same level as Luke's. She'd always hated being so tall — until now.

There was the sudden crunching of feet on the gravel path and a bang on the back door.

'Morning, sir. What's all this broken glass? More trouble here last night was there?'

The builder had arrived.

5

Tania stretched out her jeans-clad legs. They immediately collided with those of Luke's. They'd been the only customers in the dining room at The Feathers, and now they were the only occupants of the snug. She stifled a satisfied yawn and massaged the back of her neck. It had been a long day and had finished too late for her to drive back to London.

Tania had been surprised when Luke had suggested that they walk down to The Feathers and share a meal. She didn't know why she hadn't walked out on the job at first light, when she'd challenged him to dismiss her. The trouble was . . . she liked him. Although why she should like the man, she had no idea. Especially since he was high-handed, overwhelmingly arrogant and a bully, full of outdated prejudices.

Hadn't he made his views on the predatory habits of unattached females more than clear? Only a modern day dinosaur would think that a lone, unmarried female *had* to be in search of a mate! All of which meant that she had no reason to feel anything but contempt for Luke. So . . . so, why didn't she?

Another problem was that they seemed to work well together. Personal differences aside, their views and methods gelled. He understood the house, shared her feelings for it, and was responding with enthusiasm to her proposals. She could tell that like her, he was excited by the project. She'd worked with businessmen before, and all too often had found their tastes jaded. Luke was different. In fact, he was totally different from any other man she'd ever met.

'I'll book a room for tonight at The Feathers,' she'd said in reply to his dinner invitation, as she'd gathered up her notes, samples, tape measures and charts, thrusting them into her holdall.

'Not on my account, I hope,' Luke had said firmly.

He'd been outside for part of the day and had smelled of earth and wet grass — a smell which reminded Tania of her childhood and Mr Harrison. Her mouth suddenly watered at the juicy memory of the summer fruits he used to grow. Fruit didn't seem to taste the same any more, she thought with a rueful smile. She must be getting old. Maybe even policeman would soon start looking too young!

'On my own account,' Tania had insisted. There was no way she was spending a second night in her sleeping bag at The Peacock House. Her back and her nerves wouldn't stand it.

'And I'm paying half the dinner bill,' she'd added, in case he started banging on at her again, repeating his chauvinist principles about single females. He really was just out of the ark! She wished that they could be friends. However, with his hang-ups *and* the huge gull's egg lump on the back of his

108

head, things weren't looking very promising in that direction.

It also irked her that even after their rocky reintroduction last night, they actually seemed to share the same sense of humour. She'd particularly appreciated the wicked parody as Luke had imitated the builder, who'd continually insisted that yet another job 'couldn't be done, Guv.' If Tania hadn't known better, she'd have thought that they were like old friends renewing their acquaintance; enjoying getting back together again as they shared their laughter.

Luke had proved to be an entertaining dinner companion, talking about gardening, sixties music and his Harley Davidson — apparently the three great passions of his life. All of which had surprised her. Nothing about Luke seemed to fit. What other tycoon, in the fast-paced world of computer technology, would admit to liking gardening?

He'd changed from his work clothes into casual social clothes — jeans, polo shirt and a leather jacket. Tania suspected the total ensemble had probably cost a fortune. But he also had some earth under his fingernails, a legacy from having spent some part of the afternoon scratching around in an old rose bed. He was proving to be a very difficult man to classify.

'Would you like a nightcap?'

'Mmm, yes please. Maybe a glass of Chardonnay?'

It was cool and clear, just how Tania liked it. And then, as if on cue, strains of Mozart's music drifted through from the dining room.

'It's not Friday, is it?' she asked as Luke caught her on a satisfied sigh.

'What's so special about Fridays?' he asked.

'Nothing. It's just that on Friday nights, I like to listen to Mozart and have a glass of Chardonnay. It's a sort of ritual with me. And if you make any wisecracks about 'old maids' getting set in their ways, I'll . . . '

'Would I?' he taunted, with a

buccaneer smile on his lips which had Tania's red corpuscles racing.

Her fingers hovered over the sparkling contents of her glass. She'd never been the slightest bit tempted to throw wine over a man — not until now, anyway. But neither had she ever clobbered a man on the back of the head with a torch — until last night! So, what was it about Luke which was making her act so completely out of character?

'Truce . . . ?' he murmured, giving her his buccaneer smile once again.

God! He would have made an amazing pirate, Tania told herself, having difficulty disguising the shivers shooting up and down her spine. She could just imagine him swinging a cutlass, splicing the main brace — or whatever it was that pirates did. Unfortunately, she'd never been good at studying history in school.

'Truce.' Tania agreed with relief. 'That poached salmon, plus blackberry tart and cream, has left me feeling fat and lazy. I haven't got the energy to fight with you.'

'You have a healthy appetite, haven't you?'

'So have you,' she retorted, having watched him demolish a generous portion of new potatoes.

'Shuna used to peck at a few bits of salad and declare herself fit to burst.'

Tania felt as though she were skating on thin ice. If she moved it would crack under her feet. 'Shuna?'

'My ex-wife.'

'I see.' Tania waited very carefully, stifling all personal emotion at this nugget of information which he'd just dropped gratuitously into her lap. To say anything at this point might be a mistake. He'd obviously been married. So, who was she? Where was she?

'She's a model . . . ' Luke answered her first unspoken question.

'A model?' Tania felt a stupid stab of disappointment. In her time she'd had to work with several media types and, almost without exception, they'd been self-centred egocentrics. So, Luke Sinclair was a media wannabe? The thought left an unpleasant taste in Tania's mouth.

'I didn't say that *I* was a model.' There was a sudden, angry glint in Luke's eyes, 'So you can wipe that expression of disgust off your face.'

Tania flinched as if he'd actually slapped her face. 'I . . . um . . . ' she stumbled to a stop. What on earth was she supposed to say? He was quite right, of course. It was absolutely none of her business who he was or wasn't married to. Shuna . . . that was an unusual name. Shuna Sinclair . . . ? It had a short of sibilant hiss to it. And then Tania caught her breath on a sharp gasp.

Of course — *Shuna S*! How could she have been so dense? The model's face was plastered across the front of just about every celebrity magazine going. And now she remembered where she'd seen Luke Sinclair, and why he'd appeared so familiar. There'd been a series of in-depth articles on him and his wife: 'The Golden Couple Split', in just about all the glossy magazines.

'Sorry . . . ' Tania quickly waved a hand in the air. 'I didn't mean to interrupt.'

'You've obviously heard the name?'

In the dying embers of the fire, Luke's eyes seemed to have changed from their normal deep blue. They were now almost black with despair. There was nothing of the entertaining after-dinner companion about him now.

'Who hasn't?' She tried to keep her own voice upbeat.

Shuna S was one of the elite band of super-models, the face of 'Millennium', a range of cosmetics designed for the new century. The Sunday newspapers had gained a lot of mileage out of the story, and the subsequent marriage break-up. A lot of dirt had been dished up about their private life, although Tania hadn't bothered to read it. That kind of tabloid tackiness left her feeling sick.

'Do you read the newspapers?'

'I did see . . . er . . . something about the break up,' she confessed. There was no point in lying about that, especially since it had been given mega media coverage.

Luke sipped his drink and banged it back down on to the table. 'I would have thought that the gutter press was hardly your choice of reading matter.' His voice was as cold as the ice clinking in his glass.

'I only read the gossip columns for professional reasons. It helps me to keep in touch with the trends of the rich and famous.' Tania hated having to justify herself — especially to someone like Luke. It was a part of her job which she didn't particularly relish, but it had to be done.

'Then you'll also know that my wife left me, and the reason why she did so?'

Tania shifted uncomfortably in the squashy leather chair.

'You really don't have to go on,' she muttered, wishing that she'd never speculated about his personal life. Most people were only too pleased to talk about themselves, but their lives hadn't been splashed across the more lurid sections of the Press in nauseating detail. Tania had been sickened by the whole affair, and really hadn't read much about it. But no one, unless they'd been living on another planet could fail to recognise the face of 'Millennium'.

Luke didn't appear to be listening to her. From where she was sitting, Tania could hear the raw pain in his voice as he said, 'Xavier. He's the lead singer with Zorro. They're now living in the South of France.'

The last of the logs in the fire spat noisy sparks in their direction. Glad of the distraction, she picked up the poker and prodded the hot embers. Another shower of sparks created a miniature fireworks display, before she placed more logs on to the fire.

She stole a look at Luke's profile. The flames licking the new logs cast his face into an eerie light. There was no sign of the teasing, laughing man who'd mocked her for wearing elephant pyjamas, or laughed when her hair had tumbled down in disarray.

This was a man whose heart had, quite simply, been broken in two. She wanted to put out a hand and touch the sadness on his face. She wanted to tell him that she understood, that she knew what it was to lose the only person in the world whom you had ever loved; to have your heart torn from you in the twinkling of an eye — a moment that would forever remain indelibly etched on your soul. But she couldn't. It was private territory and she would be trespassing.

'The break-up is one of the reasons why I'm moving back to England. I need a base here. The house in the States is being sold.'

Shuna S must have hurt Luke badly, she thought, feeling a stab of sadness at a marriage which had gone so badly wrong. She'd lost Harry, but there had been no bitter words or degrading visits to solicitors.

So, Luke was selling up Stateside to come back to Little Chipping. It might seem a strange choice of place for a refuge, but the villagers kept themselves to themselves and even the most persistent newshound would never find out that he owned The Peacock House. The villagers would quite simply close their doors on the Press.

'I'm so sorry,' Tania felt the inadequacy of her words the moment she spoke them.

'For what?'

'Your w-wife . . . ' she stammered.

'I have no wife,' he said firmly, rising to his feet and walking over to the window, staring out into the darkness.

With a helpless shrug of her shoulders, Tania sipped her wine. Just as soon as she could, she was intending to make her excuses and go up to her room. Apart from anything else, she had some last-minute notes to go through.

'Where are you going to sleep tonight?' she asked as he came back to the table and stood staring down into the fire. 'I mean, which room? In The Peacock House? Or . . . um . . . or are you going to use The Lodge?'

Unfortunately, her attempt to change the topic of conversation was clearly sounding all wrong. Heaven knows what he was making of her attempt to bring the evening to a civilised close.

In fact, he was now regarding her with an extremely odd expression on his face. But, even as she tried to puzzle out what he was really thinking, his next words turned her world upside down.

'I could always spend the night here.'

Steady! Tania told herself quickly. Don't go over the top on this one.

'I got the last room,' she said with a determinedly pleasant smile, before the next moment she felt her face freezing into a mask.

'So . . . ?'

Tania swallowed her wine so quickly

that it caught at the back of her throat.

'What on earth . . . ?' she spluttered, her eyes watering.

'Not making myself clear?'

Tania knew that her face was flaming beetroot red, and that it would probably give Luke more amusement and ammunition, but she didn't care. 'If you mean what I think you mean . . . ?'

'Yes, I do. Here, in the glow of the firelight, you're looking warm, comfortable and particularly beautiful. So, of course I want to make love to you.'

Tania put down her glass, ignoring the rest of her Chardonnay.

'My suggestion doesn't seem to have gone down too well.'

'You know where you can stick your suggestion!'

His lips twitched with amusement. 'That's a 'no' then, is it?'

'Too damned right!' she snapped. 'It's 'no commitment' — remember? Your rules, or had they slipped your memory?'

Don't do this to me! a silent voice

howled inside Tania's head, as the left-hand side of her brain — the one with all the primitive urges — fought a losing battle with the right-hand, sensible side.

'No chance that you'll change your mind?'

Tania had the horrible suspicion that he was playing with her emotions, just to see how far she would go.

'It'll be a no, until . . . until . . . ' Her lips didn't seem able to frame the words properly, and Tania realised to her horror that she must have drunk far too much, since she simply couldn't come up with the right words.

'*No!* No more . . . ' she protested, her hand quickly clasping hold of his, in an attempt to prevent him from topping up her glass. His skin was firm and so . . . so masculine to touch, that it seemed to send her body into overdrive.

'Until the peacocks return to The Peacock House?'

It wasn't fair, she told herself miserably. It simply wasn't fair that

Luke should be so gut-wrenchingly beddable. Was 'beddable' a proper word? She didn't know and, quite frankly, she didn't care! Harry had been no more than a boy, with soft unformed features, while Luke Sinclair was a man. A man she wanted to sleep with. A man, moreover, who'd just had precisely the same idea. A man whom she'd just turned down — an action which the insane part of her psyche knew that she was going to bitterly regret for the rest of her life.

'Until . . . until the peacocks return,' she repeated the words, liking the idea. The image of sapphire peacocks, strutting brazenly across their lawns as they'd done in the past, brought a soft curve of memory to her lips.

Luke gave as low rumble of laughter. 'You're a romantic at heart,' he murmured, putting out a hand to touch her cheek. 'With a nose which goes pink when you're outraged — and red when you're really angry. I bet that you love rainbows in puddles, and sunsets too.'

'Sunrises,' Tania croaked. Heavens! He really knew how to press the right buttons. She couldn't take much more of this. Any minute now, she'd be ripping off her blouse — and goodness knows what else!

With practised ease, Luke was now slowly moving his finger over her cheek, on down the side of her face, softly touching her lips before gently stroking her nose. Tania didn't care if it was shining like a beacon. By now, she was ready to accept any proposal he put before her.

Luke's eyelashes flickered as he softly caressed the side of her face. He was well aware of the fact that he shouldn't have come on to Tania quite so strongly, but he hadn't been able to help himself. She was so unconsciously beautiful, it was more than he could take. In fact, this situation was swiftly becoming far more difficult than he'd planned. He hadn't bargained on falling in love with her — again — so quickly, or so completely.

'If you're really not going to take me up on my offer . . . ' With a superhuman control of his masculinity he affected a languid drawl. 'Then I think that I'd better get back to my lonely vigil.' Luke abruptly removed his hand. 'I'll see you in the morning. Call for me at The Lodge, about nine o'clock.'

'What? No . . . wait!'

Tania was going mad. Luke couldn't walk out on her now — not like this. She'd die of disappointment. It wasn't easy struggling out of the wing-backed chair. By the time she'd got to the door of The Feathers, Luke was already striding through the cool evening air along the river path, his broad shoulders flexing as he thrust his hands into his pockets.

'Luke . . . ' she called out, her voice carrying clearly in the still night air.

He half-turned, hesitated, then waved his arm. 'I'll see you in the morning. Don't be late.' He paused, before throwing her a long lingering smile, which left Tania feeling that she'd somehow been seduced.

Her head reeling, she watched him turn away from her and walk on down the narrow path. His name caught in her throat and she had to clench her teeth to stop herself calling after him again. Her heartbeat wouldn't stop pounding in her ears. What on earth was she going to do now? Against every one of her strict principles, it looked as if she'd fallen in love with a client — a client who was still in love with his ex-wife! A client, what's more, whom she'd known for less than a week. Had her world gone mad?

The church bell rang eleven o'clock. Feeling as if she'd aged ten years in ten minutes, Tania staggered upstairs to her single room under the eaves. She was dog-tired as she fell into bed, but she didn't sleep a wink.

★ ★ ★

Clumps of purple violets nestled round the base of the water trough, jewels in a crown of functional grey metal. Tania needed the walk to clear her head of too much wine and no sleep. Umbels of wild chervil swayed in the morning breeze and a procession of ducks quacked and paddled vigorously up the stream. She went the long way round. Although her present footwear was practical, she wasn't prepared to chance the bridge a second time.

In the small hours of the morning, she'd come to the conclusion that Luke Sinclair was a Grade A rat. Shuna had chucked him, and so would she — if she got half a chance to do so. It would only take just one more repeat performance, along the lines of the previous evening, and she'd definitely take to the hills. And that decision wasn't open to negotiation. As far as she was concerned, she was merely here to do a job. And she was going to make sure that Luke paid a double premium for her services. In fact, she wished now that she'd laid him out cold with her torch. Perhaps that might have knocked some sense into his head!

With these thoughts whirling round her head, Tania reached The Lodge at exactly nine o'clock. A zippy white sports car, sporting French number plates, was parked on the hard standing next to Luke's Ferrari. Intrigued, Tania rang the bell and waited. She was just about to ring again, when the door was opened by the most stunningly beautiful woman she had ever seen.

'Hello . . . ' The sleepy Eurasian eyes were almond-shaped and such a vivid green that they made Tania blink.

The woman gave her a lazy smile. 'You must be Tania,' she added, her voice a mixture of cultured English vowels and a slight trace of a transatlantic accent. 'We've been expecting you. Come in. Luke's not up yet. You kept him working far too hard yesterday.' She wagged a playful finger at Tania. 'I'll have to keep an eye on the pair of you.'

On autopilot, Tania found herself following her through into a small living room. She was wearing white leather trousers and a brilliant pink T-shirt, which couldn't have been a greater contrast to Tania's chain-store shirt and jeans with grass stains down the front, from where she'd helped Luke in the rose garden, the day before.

Tania was aware of the other woman's eyes taking in every detail of her appearance.

'I'm sorry,' she gave a tinkling little laugh. 'I haven't introduced myself. I'm Shuna Sinclair.'

The introduction had been unnecessary. Tania had recognised her the moment that she'd opened the front door. A slow furnace smouldered inside her. So this was the wife . . . ex-wife . . . whom Luke claimed was no longer a part of his life!

'I would offer you coffee, but we're not really up and running yet. I only arrived last night.'

Shuna was now moving about the

room with darting little movements, plumping up cushions on the two makeshift chairs, which Tania and Luke had hastily brought down from The Peacock House the night before, on their way to The Feathers.

'And Luke was so late back from the pub,' Shuna continued. 'It really was too bad of him. He knew that I was coming. Oh, dear . . . ' She put a delicate hand to her mouth, stifling an embarrassed little laugh. 'I'm forgetting, of course. He was with you, wasn't he?' Tania could feel her rage turning crimson. 'It's so like him to do that. He knows that I get jealous very easily.' The almond eyes looked at Tania's stained jeans and over-large shirt. 'Still . . . yours is only a business arrangement, isn't it? So there's no need for me to become too possessive.'

Tania wanted to explode. Luke had used her. It was obvious that he'd wanted to pay Shuna back for running off with Xavier. And what better way, than to try and seduce the nearest female to hand? And to think that she'd very nearly given in! What a fool she'd been. If she could find Luke's secateurs, she'd take great pleasure in using them on him — right now!

'And then, of course, we were so late getting to sleep . . . ' Shuna's ivory skin turned dusky pink. She left the sentence unfinished, but Tania more than caught her drift.

'Luke's clearly not ready,' she said, ignoring Shuna's satisfied little snigger. 'So I'll go on up to the house.'

She certainly had no wish to stay here, listening to Shuna telling her all about the night which the other woman had spent with Luke. She might just throw up. How *could* she have let her heart be duped by a two-timing, son of a . . .

'I think we've got some orange juice . . . ' Shuna muttered, clearly still intent on playing the good hostess.

'I'll get on. There's plenty of work to do.' As she spoke, Tania could hear the sound of someone moving about upstairs. It had to be Luke. And since the little lodge only had one bedroom — what further proof did she need that Luke and Shuna had spent the night together? 'I'll be up at the house if Luke needs me.'

'We may be going out later,' Shuna said, opening the door for Tania, who caught a whiff of the other woman's perfume as she passed by. Possibly Jasmine . . . ? Or some other scent, too sickly sweet for the English countryside.

Tania was glad to get out into the fresh air, anger fuelling her pace as she strode rapidly up the drive towards The Peacock House. She was glad that there was no one around to see her. She knew that she looked mad, muttering wildly to herself, hair undone and hands balled into shadow boxing fists. Just wait until she saw Luke Sinclair. He wouldn't know what had hit him!

Reaching the top sweep of the carriage drive, she found the golden stone working its familiar magic. From this angle, the newly cleaned, diamond-paned windows sparkled in the morning sun, and the rose beds had responded to yesterday's mini-makeover. It would break her heart to say goodbye, but she had to get this job over as quickly as possible. And then it would be back to Camden and the security of her studio and her solitary Friday nights. And to hell with Luke Sinclair!

6

'This will take some doing.' The contractor consulted his plans. 'The penalty clause is a bugger. I mean, how on earth does he expect us to finish in the timescale he's given us?'

'I'll be upstairs if you need me.' Tania was in no mood to listen to his problems. She had quite enough of her own.

The builder's whistling grated on her nerves as she stormed upstairs, still seething with anger, closing the door of the master bedroom carefully behind her. After all, whatever had happened certainly wasn't the fault of the house, and there was no point in needlessly damaging the fixtures and fittings. She ran a hand lovingly over the faded paintwork. Well, at least the house was pleased to see her.

Tania took a deep breath, before

crossing the room and unlatching the large glass windows leading out on to a balcony which had seen better days. She gazed at the rolling hills in the distance, studiously ignoring The Lodge nestling innocently at the gates. Sunlight slanted across the dew-studded lawn. The sight of nature in all its natural glory never failed to calm her. Working close to the environment was one of the most satisfying challenges of her job, and already she was beginning to feel recharged.

There was no point in wasting any more time on Luke Sinclair. She had a job to do, and the sooner she got on with it — the sooner that he, his dazzling blue eyes and lazy smile would be out of her life.

She worked intently for several hours, only pausing to drink a quick cup of tea with the builder.

'It's gonna be quite something,' he'd said with reluctant approval. 'Nice to see the house coming back to its former glory. Been empty far too long. Take this room here . . . ' he added, gesturing around Tania's favourite room: the big drawing room with the double doors leading out on to the crazy paving patio, and on down to the peacock lawn.

'It will look lovely with the floor restored and all polished up,' the builder continued. 'That Mr Sinclair wants nothing modern. All like it used to be. Got plans for the garden, too. It's always been a family house. Have you heard that he means to settle down?' Tania had nodded. 'With his lady friend — his ex-wife by all accounts — model or something. Bit of a modern arrangement. Still . . . ' he sniffed, 'it seems that anything goes these days.'

Tania had picked up her tea and gone back upstairs. She'd explode if she heard any more about Luke's plans. And how come even the wretched builder knew about them, before she did?

She tried to immerse herself in colour charts, swatches and her sketches, but her mind wasn't on the job. No wonder Luke Sinclair had been reluctant to employ her. She was single and, to all intents and purposes, seemingly available. However accommodating his ex-wife, she wouldn't want another female about the place when she was busy rebuilding a broken marriage. And to think that Tania had been stupid enough to believe him, when he'd said that marriage didn't figure on his agenda. *Of course, it didn't*! He was already married — or as good as.

Had Luke Sinclair told her one word of truth? Was he even a businessman with his own computer business? Hadn't Ellie said that Charles couldn't find anything out about him? With these thoughts raging round her head, she didn't hear the gentle tap on the door.

'Tania?' There was a smell of jasmine. Shuna hesitated on the threshold. 'Not disturbing you, am I?'

'No. Come in.' Tania stretched her

aching back, 'I've almost finished up here.'

Shuna was now dressed in an emerald-green blouse, the exact colour of her eyes, and the tightest pair of red leather pants which Tania had ever seen. For her part, Tania was looking even grubbier now, than a few hours ago when she'd first met Shuna, having crawled round the floor and climbed up ladders taking measurements. Putting her hand to her hair, her fingers found remnants of a spider's web nestling in her topknot. Shuna's hair was dark, sleek and straight, not a mass of heavy curls that wouldn't behave. Tania couldn't imagine any dirt even daring to land on Shuna's shining hair.

'Luke's gone to visit his mother, so I thought I'd come up and see how you're getting on.'

'His mother?' Tania stopped searching her hair for surplus spiders.

'She lives in a neighbouring village. Didn't you know?'

Tania shook her head. There was no

reason for her to know. So why did she feel unsettled as she added another fact to the ever-growing list of things she didn't know about Luke Sinclair? Luke hadn't mentioned anything about having a mother in the area — not even when Tania had told him about her past relationship with Harry. Already she was beginning to regret that lapse. She'd always made it a rule never to talk about herself and Harry.

'I didn't go with him,' Shuna said, moving about the room with petite movements. 'Things are a bit difficult between us,' she added, screwing up her pert little nose. 'Luke's mother is old-fashioned and never really approved of me. She thought that he should have settled down with a local girl. She also wasn't too happy when we split. Silly really . . . but anyway, I'm back now — for good.'

Tania turned back to her sketchpad not wanting to hear any more. She had a mountain of work to get through and hoped that Shuna wouldn't stay long.

'So, what are you doing there?' Shuna asked, peering over Tania's shoulder.

'Calculations, mapping out ideas. Trying to see what works and what doesn't.'

Tania hoped her voice didn't sound too tight. She'd been such a fool and now she was paying the price — with interest! How Luke Sinclair must have laughed at her behind her back last night. There was a sharp snap. Tania was dismayed to see that she had broken her pencil in two. She'd like to have snapped a part of Luke Sinclair in two, as well.

She'd always been in control of her own destiny and didn't like being cast as a victim in some elaborate role-play between Luke and his estranged wife. She straightened her shoulders. She was blowed if she was going to start now. Luke Sinclair was to blame for this ghastly situation — even if they'd both been victims of Ellie's overkill. He couldn't be allowed to get away with

. . . what? That was the pain of it. He hadn't physically done anything to her.

'Can I see?'

'There isn't much to see,' Tania said, forcing a smile and holding out her pad of hieroglyphics.

Shuna's sloe eyes blinked over Tania's much-scored notes, then round the room.

'This is the main bedroom, isn't it?' With a little smile, Shuna walked to the window. 'It'll be lovely to have breakfast on the balcony in the summer.'

There was such an unpleasant taste in Tania's mouth, she felt as though she'd swallowed the spiders, as well as their web. Shuna was clearly intending to share this room — with Luke.

'I see it decorated as an eastern temple, with rich brocade in gold and magenta,' Shuna told her. 'We'll have gold fittings in the bathroom, and thick deep pile carpets of rich burgundy. As for the bed . . . ?' She pursed her pouting lips, putting her head to one side in deep thought, before happily

140

clapping her hands together. 'Yes! A canopy over the top. In pink . . . and pink linen on the bed itself.'

'You can't!' Tania gasped, utterly horrified, and all thoughts of revenge on Luke swept aside as she listened to Shuna's plans.

'Why not?' There was no trace of the compliant oriental about Shuna now. Her eyes were narrowed and glittering. 'It's my bedroom.'

'But Luke and I discussed what we had in mind . . . '

'Mr Sinclair and I will decide on the decoration of our own bedroom ourselves.'

'But . . . '

'There are no buts about it. Who do you think is financing this project?'

'I was given to understand that it was Luke.' If Shuna S was her paymaster, then the project was clearly doomed. Golden temples and gilded bed canopies were not items she could work with.

'He will, of course, have a say over

the decoration of certain areas of the house, but I have the final word.'

Tania was seething. Shuna would appear to belong to that select band of models, who wouldn't get out of bed for less than an astronomical sum of money. And now she was clearly intending to squander some of her inflated fees on a monument to Bad Taste. She was also displaying all the temperament of a diva of the catwalk. Which might be fine in Milan, but this was Little Chipping! Tania wasn't temperamental, but she was capable of fighting as dirty as the next woman — particularly when it concerned her work.

'I was employed by Luke . . . Mr Sinclair,' she said firmly. If that was how Shuna wanted to play it then Tania could go along with it. 'He never mentioned your involvement.'

'That was before I came back.'

'If you're dispensing with my services, I need to hear it from him and not second hand.' Tania tossed her head, sending a couple of spiders flying through the air. 'There will, of course, be a substantial cancellation fee,' she added for good measure.

Her words clearly had an effect on Shuna, who was all smiles again. Tania couldn't believe someone could change expressions so quickly. Tricks of the trade she thought sourly then silently berated herself for sounding such a rat bag.

'I'm sure that we can come to a compromise,' the model murmured. 'Naturally Luke has his own ideas, but when I discuss mine with him, I know that he'll want to do it my way. He always has in the past.'

My God, thought Tania, she's serious!

'What about the builders . . . the plans for the garden . . . ? You can't change everything. We've already started the work.' Tania thought with dismay about the contractor downstairs, busy ordering materials and engaging extra men.

'We'll see. In the garden, I thought of perhaps having a themed setting. Maybe a lily pond and a Japanese bridge . . . ?' She smiled prettily. 'I know English people like ponds with little statues. We could have a pretend heron, perhaps, or one of those frogs . . . '

Tania thought that she was going mad. 'Luke wants to keep it unspoilt,' she said firmly, although Shuna didn't seem to be listening to her.

'I like garden ornaments,' Shuna insisted stubbornly.

Tania could feel her mouth being stretched in an unnatural smile. It was only with the greatest difficulty that she stopped herself screaming with laughter as she suddenly thought of the peacocks. They'd sweep aside any garden ornament with an aristocratic flick of their elevated tails. Tania closed her eyes remembering how, beautiful as they were, the peacocks had been no respecters of the Fitzroys' croquet lawn or tennis court. They'd strolled at will, confident in their kingdom and displaying their fine feathers — and to hell with everyone else! Tania refused to draw a parallel with Shuna Sinclair, although she was sorely tempted.

'What about the peacocks?'

'Luke wants peacocks?' Shuna said, swivelling back to face Tania, eyes alight with sudden interest. Tania sensed mischief. How could she have ever thought that Shuna's eyes were beautiful? In their depths was something that made her want to shudder. An overdose of Shuna could make her feel unwell.

'In the old peacock garden,' Tania admitted reluctantly. 'They used to roam at will.'

Shuna snapped her fingers. 'I think I can help. A model friend of mine . . . '

'Shouldn't we talk to Luke first?' Tania said quickly. Much as she hated the idea, she needed to talk to talk to Luke — as soon as possible. And then, if he didn't like what she was saying, she was intending to get out of here with the speed of light. As far as she

145

was concerned, Luke and his wife richly deserved each other.

'He won't be back until later this afternoon,' Shuna told her, suddenly turning towards the door. 'See you,' she added, and then was gone, leaving only a faint trace of jasmine in the air.

In a fit of fury, Tania delved in her bag for her mobile and punched out Ellie's number. If it hadn't been for her sister, she wouldn't have got herself into this mess in the first place. In fact, this was the last . . . absolutely the very last time she allowed Ellie to interfere in her life. From now on, they would go separate ways. And if Ellie didn't like it — tough. She glanced at her watch. One o'clock. Good. Ellie would be having lunch.

'Hi? This is . . . Whoops. Sorry.' Ellie's voice cut in on the answer phone. 'I'm here. This is the real me. What? Tania?' she screeched. 'Where've you been? I've been trying to get you for ages.'

'I'm at The Peacock House.'

'Great. How's it going?'

'It isn't.'

'Tania. You're the pits. You haven't . . . '

'I haven't done anything. Did you know this precious Luke Sinclair of yours was married to a model called Shuna S?'

'What? You're kidding. The one who ran off with a pop star? That lead singer, or is it a guitarist? The one with snake hips and . . . '

'Spare me the details.'

'Something wrong? You sound a bit cross.'

'Sometimes Ellie I could wring your neck. This is all your fault.'

'What is?'

'This business with Luke. You knew . . . '

'I didn't know anything. Tania, there's no need to be angry with me. I'm sorry. You know I only want you to be happy. I thought this was an opportunity not to be missed when Luke mentioned that he was buying The Peacock House.'

Tania snatched at her hair and a few more bits of cobweb came away. She didn't doubt Ellie's motives, but she wasn't going to let her off the hook yet.

'You knew that he had connections in the area?'

'Has he?' Ellie sounded puzzled. 'No I didn't know. I thought that he was returning from the States. Something to do with his computer business ... I don't know. Anyway, he needed an interior designer and I recommended you. Tania ... ?'

Tania was only half listening. She could feel a ridiculous lump rising in her throat. She'd so badly wanted this job, and now it was being snatched away from her by circumstances outside her control. It had been a dream come true, but in the space of one morning it had all gone pear-shaped — all because of blasted Luke Sinclair and his equally atrocious ex-wife. Why had he strung her along? He must have known that Shuna was coming back. And to think that, last night, she'd been close to making the biggest blunder of her life.

'Tania. I'm sorry, really I am. Don't go all quiet on me.'

Tania could never stay angry with Ellie for long. Infuriating as her sister was, she meant well.

'Did Charles find anything out about Luke?' Tania asked in a flat voice, not holding out much hope.

'Funny you should mention that,' Ellie bubbled back. 'He's drawn a blank. He's looked him up in some sort of company record book, or whatever. He's got business collateral, but that's about it. I thought his face looked familiar though and, when he mentioned that he knew your work, I suppose that I just assumed you knew him as well.' After a pause Ellie added, 'Are things going really badly?'

'His ex-wife's come back with ideas of her own. It looks like all my designs are going down the pan.'

'Darling, I'm so sorry.' Ellie was all sympathy. 'You know I wouldn't have had this happen for the world. You're the best, you know that. You don't need some little tramp walking all over you. Do you want me to come up? Fight your quarter?'

Tania felt a warm wetness at the back of her eyes. Good old Ellie. She may drive her mad, but she could be relied on to champion Tania's cause. Let anyone upset her big sister and she'd be there to take on all comers — all five foot and seven stone of her!

'It's not your fault, Sis. Sorry I sounded off just now. I was so bugged.'

One thing about Ellie, she was never one to bear a grudge. 'It didn't happen,' she said airily. 'When are you coming back?'

'I've got to see Luke, but he's out for the day . . . '

'Come straight down here. I'll send Charles and the boys to his mother. She loves having them. Without me, she can rule the roost — you know how bossy she is.' Tania smiled down the line. Ellie and her mother-in-law were two of a kind. 'We can spend a girly weekend together.'

'I'll do my best, but I'm not promising anything.'

Tania felt better after her call to Ellie. Even when they had rows, Ellie was the only constant in Tania's life. She didn't doubt for one moment her sister would always be there for her. But this was one mess she needed to sort out for herself without any sisterly support.

Tania began throwing her work into her bag. There was nothing more she could do here for the moment — if at all. She meant what she'd said about a hefty cancellation fee for this fiasco. When she thought of all the work she'd turned down, she wanted to scream. She took a deep breath. She must focus on the positive, not the negative, otherwise she'd be climbing the wall.

She shuddered at the thought of what Shuna would do to the master bedroom, and was glad she was leaving. It would bring tears to her eyes to see the wonderful master suite turned into some sort of oriental brothel keeper's bedroom.

Calling out good-bye to the builder, Tania walked slowly down the drive. There was no sign of Luke's Ferrari or Shuna's car. At the gates, she turned to take one last look at The Peacock House bathed in early afternoon sun. Then, with a heavy heart, she began her slow walk back to The Feathers.

It was late by the time she finally drove her hatchback back into The Feathers' car park. A visit to Cheltenham had proved very productive and the back of the car was loaded up with fresh samples, catalogues, charts and some shopping. It was so rare for her to have a free afternoon that she grabbed the chance whenever she could.

Staggering to reception and blinking the late afternoon sun from her eyes, Tania didn't immediately see the tall figure lounging by the desk.

'Retail therapy?' The lazy question sent her pent-up anger fizzing all over the place.

'I don't know how you dare show your face, you lying, double-cross-ing . . . '

'Whoa, hold on!' Now her eyes had adjusted to the gloomy interior of The Feathers, Tania could see that Luke was looking amused as usual.

'You can wipe that smirk off your face, I'm not in the mood to be pleasant. Don't you realise what you've done? You've made a big mistake this time, Buster.' She dropped one of her sample books on the floor, and saw with great pleasure that it had landed on Luke's foot. She could only hope that it had broken several of his toes!

'You look rather hot, Tania. Would you care for some tea? Or a drink in the bar? And don't worry,' he added, clearly having no problem in reading her mind. 'My foot's fine.' He removed the fallen book and placed it on a convenient chair.

'Pity!' she snapped. 'No tea, thank you. I'd rather drink tea with . . . '

'Don't say it.' His lips were twitching

with laughter and Tania, to her horror, found herself longing to feel their touch on hers. 'There are several ladies of advanced years in the conservatory!'

'Will you let me pass?' She made to go by him.

'Not until you agree to have dinner with me.'

'It would choke me.'

'Here. Just the two of us. I see they've got John Dory on the menu. Have you ever had it? It's a delicious fish. It's got a fingerprint on the side — some sort of biblical connection, I believe. Of course, with your healthy appetite, you'll probably need two portions. Then there's new potatoes and fresh . . . '

'Why don't you have dinner with your wife?' she asked grimly. 'Or had her presence here completely slipped your memory?'

Luke's eyelids flickered and the expression on his face seemed to tighten, giving Tania a feeling of deep satisfaction. It looked as if her words had hit the target — spot on! 'We need to talk about Shuna.'

'Oh, no, we don't!'

'Yes. We do.'

'OK. We'll talk now.'

'At dinner,' Luke said firmly.

'No.' Tania was equally firm. By now they were attracting the passing attention of other guests.

'If you don't have dinner with me . . . ' Luke said, deliberately raising his voice, 'I'll have my dinner here, alone, and join you in your room after coffee.'

Tania looked round self-consciously. Everyone in the confined reception area could now hear every word they were saying to one another. She was quite certain that he was doing it on purpose, and also making a great show of looking at his watch. 'That should be about half past ten,' he added loudly. 'If you like, we can spend the night together.'

'I'm definitely *not* staying the night!' Tania cut him short, trying to ignore the knowing smiles beginning to show on the faces of their eavesdroppers.

'You're going to have to.' Swiftly, so that even Tania didn't see him move, Luke snatched her car keys from the reception desk.

'Give them back to me.'

'I'm serious, Tania.' There was none of the laughing cavalier about Luke now. 'We do need to talk. I've booked a room here tonight as well . . . '

'You've done what? Where's Shuna?'

'At The Lodge.'

'Then that's where you should be.'

'Will you believe me when I tell you we are not an item?'

'No.'

'Why not?'

'Frankly, I don't believe anything you say any more. You're obviously one of those people who can't tell truth from fiction.'

He eased away from the desk and came towards her. Luke was now so close to her that she could almost feel his sexuality throbbing through her veins. She didn't know what was happening to her. Except, that she had to get away from here before she found herself in real trouble.

'Please, Tania, will you have dinner with me? I don't lie, and I meant every word I said last night.' He lowered his dark head towards her, until his lips were almost touching her ear. 'Especially, what I said about wanting to make love to you.'

Tania wasn't sure, but she may have whimpered. If he carried on like this, she was clearly in danger of losing total control. She dropped the rest of her parcels on to the floor, the silken cord of her dress box being the last to slip through her unresisting fingers.

'I . . . ' The expression in Luke's eyes was making her dizzy.

'Please. I promise to behave. Just as long as you don't keep on looking at me like that — and that you also wear your new dress.'

It had been a last minute, totally impulsive purchase, which Tania had regretted the moment she'd signed the credit card slip. It would probably take up the entire horrendous cancellation fee, which she intended charging on this job.

'How did you know about my new dress?'

'Well . . . ' he drawled lightly. 'I rather think that the box has just fallen on my foot!'

Not really knowing what she was doing, Tania found herself raising a hand to Luke's face, impelled by overwhelming desire to touch the quirk tugging the corner of his lips. He held her hand to his face for a second then let her fingers fall.

'Are you trying to get me arrested for inappropriate behaviour in a public place?' he asked, bending down and picking up the dress. Not caring that they were now the focus of everybody's eyes, he held the oatmeal shantung dress against her.

'Beautiful,' he said in a voice that would have raised a glacier to boiling point. 'Wear this and keep your hair loose — after you've washed the livestock out of it, of course,' he added as, with delicate finger work, he removed some more cobwebs from her curls.

Tania wanted to snatch her dress from his other hand and stuff it back into the tissue-lined box. Instead, to her absolute disgust, she heard herself whisper, 'Eight o'clock.'

'It's a date!'

She thought that she detected a note of relief in his voice, but the collective sighs and knowing smiles from the spectators, caused her face to burn with embarrassment once again. Grabbing her parcels and refusing all offers of help to carry them upstairs, she made her get away. She needed time to be alone . . . time to think. And that meant not letting Luke anywhere near her room! Besides, there was always the possibility of being able to escape.

Unfortunately, it was only when she

closed the door behind her, that she remembered Luke still had her car keys. So she couldn't leave now, even if she wanted to.

7

Luke was seated at the bar, two glasses of champagne by his elbow.

His blue eyes darkened a shade as Tania appeared in the doorway, the tilt of her head an unmistakable silhouette. She was nervous. Not half as nervous as he was. He could have strangled Shuna — she'd nearly ruined everything with her impeccable timing. She'd always known there'd been someone else in his life, and with her unerring instinct in matters of this nature, she'd reappeared at exactly the wrong moment. Luke stood up slowly, sensing a battle. Tania Jordan wasn't going to be easy to convince.

'Never say die,' thought Tania as she squared her shoulders and walked over towards him, praying her hair wouldn't misbehave. There hadn't been much time to get ready and she'd left it damp from the shower, pinning a few tendrils back and leaving the rest to frame her face in soft chestnut curls.

However, even she had to admit that the impulse purchase of the dress had been worth the outlay. It fitted her like a dream. The oyster silk shimmered against her body movements, catching the light as her long legs moved across the room.

Luke watched her cross to the bar, desperately trying to disguise his admiration. Her elegance was natural and unspoilt, not a bit like Shuna's pouting cronies. His eyes narrowed as he noticed he wasn't the only gob-smacked male following her progress.

'Here,' he said curtly, handing her a glass and hustling her to a seat.

'What are we celebrating?' Tania squashed herself into the corner of the church-pew-type bench. The cushions were slippery on the polished oak and, try as she might, she couldn't stop herself slipping towards him.

Luke was wearing a pale blue shirt

and a tie with an enormous mauve tulip on it. The colour made Tania blink. 'Do you have a stack of those?' she pointed a cocktail stick at his tie. She'd missed lunch again and had been unable to resist the little bowl of glistening green and black olives Luke had placed in front of her.

'Our business deal and yes. I had them made up in Hong Kong.'

She could feel him moving unnecessarily closer to her. His thigh was hard against the silk of her dress. She pressed herself into the wooden back of the seat and promptly slid forward again. For once, Luke Sinclair didn't appear to find her discomfort amusing. He was looking at her so intently that she could feel the rush of blood to her face.

He held his glass up. 'Here's to us,' he said and tipped it gently towards hers.

'There is no 'us'. We don't have a deal . . . '

'Yes, we do. You agreed to undertake my commission.'

'We've got nothing in writing.'

'Handshake agreement. Trying to wriggle out of it? Because if you are . . .'

Tania felt her spine stiffen. It was gloves off time.

'If it meant never seeing you again, then I'd wriggle out of it willingly, so you can't threaten me.'

She tilted her chin and narrowed her eyes. She'd had time to reassess priorities in the shower and, if Luke Sinclair thought bullyboy tactics would work with her, he was in for a shock. She'd learned to stand on her own two feet in this business — and she wasn't about to lose her hard-won independence for the whim of some technology millionaire, who wanted to run things his way.

'You and I have different styles of business, Luke. I don't like finding I've been threatened with the sack, just on the casual word of an ex-wife . . . an ex-wife who informs me that she is the money behind the deal.'

A small muscle now quivered at the corner of Luke's mouth. It wasn't anger. It wasn't amusement. That only left . . . what? Admiration? Desire?

Tania's mouth went dry. What was wrong with her? She should be scratching Luke's eyes out, not longing to rip his shirt apart.

'You're not hearing me, Tania. I'm drinking to our ongoing contract and, despite what you think, I didn't have threats in mind, just a nice civilised arrangement. If you prefer it, I can get my legal people to cobble something together in black-and-white. Would that satisfy you?'

Tania knew she had to make a stand now, otherwise the good talking-to which she'd given herself in the shower would be on fast track to failure.

'Stop playing games Luke. You have a wife . . . '

'I have an ex-wife.'

'Whatever. It doesn't stop the chemistry working between you. What she says goes. Where does that leave me?'

Luke raised an eyebrow. 'Jealous?'

This wasn't going the way Tania had planned it.

'No, of course not. What I'm trying to say is . . . '

Luke speared an olive, and with a gut-wrenching smile he very slowly offered it to her. Before she could stop him, he was running the olive across her lips and by that simple action, had managed to prise them apart.

She winced at the sudden bite of olive, welcoming the tang of the juices in her mouth. With his thumb, Luke wiped away a trickle of moisture from the corner of her lips. There was a glint in his eyes now and a brief flash of something else.

She had seen that expression before. The day they'd first met, down by the footbridge. She hadn't known him, of course. But he'd been looking at her with a strange sense of familiarity. A memory of something stirred far back in her mind . . .

She'd been eating some summer

berries, really big extra juicy ones . . . red gooseberries, that was it . . . and there'd been someone with her and . . . and juice had dribbled down her chin on that occasion, too . . .

Tania had had these flashes before. After Harry had died, there were large gaps in her past which she couldn't seem to fill. Occasionally, something would trigger off a forgotten memory, and there'd be a quick flashback — but then, nothing. The light would go out again.

'Don't want you passing out from hunger,' he teased.

Tania hastily swallowed the olive. 'Thank you,' she managed to gasp, lecturing herself mentally to get a grip. Luke Sinclair was a clever devil but if he thought she'd be seduced by antics with an olive, he'd got another think coming.

'Where were we?' Luke's voice was tender and understanding. 'If Shuna's been spouting off, I'm sorry. It's absolute claptrap by the way. She's not the driving force behind this project. Unfortunately, she'd like to be.'

Tania could have gone on listening to him forever. It was time to break the pattern. She jerked herself back to reality. 'I understand your ex-wife's taking over. She told me you'd agree with whatever she proposed.'

'Did she?' Luke raised an eyebrow. 'What else did she say?'

'She said you always fall in with her ideas. Luke, you can't do this! She wants 'twee' lily ponds, wretched garden gnomes, and Japanese bridges. I mean, can you imagine it?' Tania's hair did a sympathy wobble as she raised agitated hands. 'Sorry,' she made a self-conscious noise. She'd gone too far again. 'I don't normally . . . '

Luke threw back his head and let out a shout of laughter. Several heads turned in the bar, female eyes lingering longest in naked curiosity, several with a tinge of envy.

'Priceless. Love to have been a fly on the wall when she told you.' He was still laughing as he picked up his champagne glass. Tania felt her heart cooling down a bit and her lips twitched reluctantly at the memory. It probably would have been different if Luke had been there to share the joke. 'Do you really think that's my style?'

'Perhaps I did over-react,' Tania admitted.

'In your place, I'd have probably been miffed too,' he admitted, touching her hand briefly with his before Tania snatched hers away.

'Where do I stand Luke?' she asked, longing to add, 'and stop looking at me like that.'

'Nothing's changed between us. Nothing professional, that is.' His eyes ran over her hair again and down to her body, leaving Tania in no doubt as to the meaning of his non-verbal communication.

'And that's the only relationship we have — a professional one.' She was glad he'd made the point. It would do no harm to endorse their status.

'Of course.' The blue eyes widened. 'Did you have anything else in mind?'

'Stop playing games, Luke. I'm immune to your . . . charm.'

'So, you find me charming?'

'It's not working, Luke.' Tania raised her hand towards the bowl of olives and then changed her mind. 'This setup. We're not working together and I have to feel empathy with my clients.'

'We were together all day yesterday.'

'And today, your ex-wife suddenly reappears, tells me she's running the show, and you disappear. What am I supposed to think?'

'There were family things I had to do. I'm sorry I wasn't there to fight your corner.'

'I don't need you for that. I just need to know my position.'

'Shuna's no threat to you.' Luke wasn't teasing her now. He looked serious as if what he was saying really mattered. 'She's back because Xavier ditched her, and that's the only reason.

She's trying to muscle in on the action here, but she'll move on.'

When he spoke like this, it was easy to believe him but Tania didn't want to be seduced by gentle words and soft memories. She wanted to carry on hating Luke Sinclair. It would be much safer for her sanity. She ignored the doubting voice in her head asking, 'Why?'

'You spent the night together. You and Shuna.' Horrified Tania raised a hand to her face. Had she really said that? It was none of her business what Luke and Shuna did. On top of everything, it made her sound possessive, the last impression she wanted to give.

'I slept on two chairs downstairs with the aid of some lumpy cushions. Remember? The ones we carried down together? I've never had such an uncomfortable night's sleep in my life. I kept thinking of the alternatives here and only iron self-control stopped me coming back. Does that answer your questions? I was having a shower when you arrived this morning and Shuna, of course, used the situation to her advantage. If you'd have waited a few minutes and given me a chance to explain, this ridiculous situation wouldn't have arisen.'

Tania's cheeks flamed from a combination of her rudeness and Luke's frankness.

'I'm not sure . . . '

'I refused to spend another night like that. Shuna hasn't left yet, so here I am. Subject closed. Fancy a spin on a Harley-Davidson after dinner?' A waiter hovered with two menus.

'Thank you. What did you say?' Tania spun back to face Luke.

'Have to change out of that dress and do something about your hair, much as I love it like that.' He tweaked a stray tendril. 'What's the matter? Idea doesn't appeal to you? Thought you were a independent girl of spirit.'

'Did you say a Harley-Davidson?'

'I did. Been over to collect it this

afternoon. Moonlight ride. Wind in your face. All that power between your legs. Easy rider. Are you on?' He looked up from his menu. 'I've only had one glass of champagne and if I promise not to drink any more, will you do me the honour of riding pillion?'

At that moment, Tania would have sat behind the second hump of a camel with him!

'Why me?' It was a stupid thing to say, but Tania wasn't into sophistication at the moment.

'Because, I just love seeing your eyes go that colour when you're mad at me — and when you're excited.'

'You're kidding.' Tania winced the moment she spoke. Why couldn't she accept compliments gracefully? Ellie would have handled this sort of thing so much better. But then, Ellie had had more practice than her older sister. From an early age, men had fallen like ninepins at Ellie's feet.

'Sort of dreamy amethyst. That day on the bridge . . . '

'I was thinking about Harry Fitzroy . . . '

Luke's lips tightened fractionally. 'The Fitzroys were fools to let you get away.'

There were forces here that Tania didn't understand. Why did the mention of Harry Fitzroy change the expression on Luke's face so radically? She looked hard at Luke and, to her amazement, realised she could no longer remember Harry's face in detail. All she could see was Luke. He filled every part of her mind and body and she realised, for the first time in her life, that she was truly in love. What she had felt for Harry had been no more than a teenage infatuation. What she felt for Luke was love of the full-blown adult variety — and the relationship, such as it was, would be equally as doomed. Luke had come out of one marriage seriously scarred. He wasn't looking for another relationship, but he was offering night rides on his Harley-Davidson.

'Yes please.' Luke's outdoor tan

deepened as he looked at her, almost convincing Tania that he'd been holding his breath.

'You mean it?'

'I'd love a ride on your Harley-Davidson,' she leaned forward and helped herself to another olive. 'And I just love the way your eyes change colour — when you're excited.' Ellie would have been proud of her delivery of that one Tania thought as she nibbled the olive.

Luke, too, seemed to be enjoying the joke.

'The noise might disturb the good residents of Little Chipping.'

Later, Tania tried to convince herself it was the champagne speaking and not the ultra-sensible, Tania Jordan, who worked with her hair in a neat pleat.

'Then let's go for it.'

'That's my girl.'

* * *

Luke had never changed his clothes so fast in his life. It had been a close call, but she'd taken the bait. He whipped off his shirt and threw it on to the bed. He'd nearly given himself away over the Fitzroys, too. Luckily, Tania hadn't picked up on that one.

Luke hopped around on one foot as he thrust a leg into his leathers. He couldn't count the number of times as a kid, when he'd wanted to throttle Harry Fitzroy. Tania only had eyes for the young son and heir, although he'd been a right little toe-rag. Grown up into an even bigger one, according to his mother.

God, she'd looked beautiful tonight in the bar. Luke zipped up his trousers and grabbed a second jacket for Tania and a helmet. She hadn't remembered yet. He hoped when she did, she wouldn't want to kill him.

He let out a sigh of relief as she came out The Feathers and into the car park. He'd half-expected her to have second thoughts. Under the security light, she looked nervous and pale but he'd soon put colour in her cheeks.

'Ready?' He handed over the helmet and jacket. 'Put these on. You'll need them.'

'It's beautiful,' Tania took in the sleek bodywork gleaming in the moonlight.

'Every one of them has a soul, so they say.'

'Where do you keep it?'

She was struggling into her jacket and didn't catch Luke's reply.

With a frown, he poked her hair up into the helmet. 'Don't suppose it'll stay there for long. Takes lessons from you, does it, in doing its own thing?' His fingers lingered on the nape of her neck. 'Not scared?'

Luke silently congratulated himself on the right taunt. She'd never admit it even if she were. Lord, he'd never wanted her as much as he did now. Here in the moonlight, scared but damned to admit it, with sapphire orbs for eyes. His body hardened. The only two things in life to turn him on were here — together — his Harley and Tania Jordan.

'Course not,' she tossed her head. One of the curls immediately escaped the helmet. His fingers tightened round it.

'Told you so,' he said gently tugging it. 'Ready?'

'Luke, do you think . . . ?'

'No time for second thoughts.'

He released her, slung a long leg over the saddle, and kicked the throttle. A powerful throb greeted his footwork. Tania, in her own jeans and Luke's jacket and helmet, hesitated then slung her leg over the pillion. Ellie would never believe this in a million years she thought, as she adjusted her body against Luke's powerful back.

'Where are we going?'

Windows were beginning to be opened, a dog barked, and one or two lights were turned on as Luke revved up. The vibrations shot up Tania's legs. With her body so close to his and the bike pumping adrenaline into every limb, she was horrified to find herself on the verge of orgasm.

'Anywhere — fast — before the locals start chucking buckets of water over us. Hold tight.'

Tania put her arms round Luke's waist. The wall of his back against hers was rock solid. Even through the leather, she could feel his muscles straining with the powerful monster as he slowly eased the brake off.

Tania bit down a scream as the motor-bike growled then roared into life, down the village street and out on to the open road.

The force of air robbed Tania's lungs of breath as Luke swerved round the late-night traffic. Lights and signs sped by in the velvet night and soon they were away from the towns and into the open countryside. Mile after mile sped away under them, as Luke manoeuvred his powerful monster with the ease of long practice. Every so often, they clipped a head of cow parsley off a hedge and night eyes were lit up in the powerful twin-beam headlights.

The scent of summer grass filled Tania's nostrils as they roared past the black silhouette of a Tudor church and over the bumpy crossing of a disused railway line. The moon was three-quarters full and painted ghostly patterns on the walls of the deserted clusters of cottages surrounding the humps of a monolithic burial ground. Behind her helmet, Tania laughed with the exhilaration of the mind-bending experience. There was no other way to travel. She'd slipped the bond of her inhibitions, gone to another planet, call it what you will. She was living. Ellie had been right — she'd grown staid before her time. Ellie wouldn't recognise her now as the sister she'd berated for being stuck in a rut. Charles would probably have a heart attack! She didn't think Luke had heard her laugh until she saw him make a thumbs-up sign over his shoulder.

They couldn't talk, but he'd got the message. She was one turned on lady.

She recognised the Milky Way and billions of pinprick stars dotted the sky like flashing diamonds winking down on to the outrageous behaviour below. The inside of Tania's thighs felt sore as her muscles gripped hold of the pillion, her mind blasting her other senses to oblivion.

She bit down a protest as Luke turned the bike round in an arc of graceful symmetry, using his arm to indicate which way she was supposed to lean. They sped back along a different route, too soon the Sportster ate up the miles down through the upper part of the village, past The Peacock House, majestic in the moonlight. In the distance, Tania heard the mournful wail of a peacock, at least she thought she heard it. Her mind had to be playing tricks. There weren't any peacocks, not now. They were yesterday. And today's bubble was about to burst too, she realised, as Luke lowered the engine speed and with a sharp turn eased the bike back into the car park of The Feathers.

Every part of her body was trembling as she dismounted. She struggled with her helmet, as Luke locked the bike in an old shed at the back and walked slowly back to her. In his helmet and leathers, he looked like a being from another planet.

'Take it off,' she tapped his visor, unable to stop the enormous smile stretching her face. 'That was fantastic.'

From behind the safety of his visor, he drew in his breath. There was a painful ache too in the groin of his leathers. Thankfully Tania wouldn't notice, he thought, as he slowly removed his own helmet and tried to smile as normally as possible at the girl he'd loved since she'd been a leggy teenager in shorts, picking fruit in a summer garden with juice dribbling down her face. Before he realised what she intended, she'd flung her arms round him and kissed him. His heartbeat soared, but she'd moved away from him before he could cash in on the experience.

'Thank you.' She was still smiling broadly then suddenly she wrinkled her nose and backed off. 'Yuk. You smell of oil and sweat.'

Luke didn't move. He couldn't. If she hadn't objected to his smell, he'd have been in danger of making love to her on the ground of the car park of The Feathers — and that really would have given the inhabitants of Little Chipping something to chuck their buckets of water over!

'We'd better go up,' he said in a voice that wasn't his own, at least he didn't recognise it. 'And don't make too much noise,' he cautioned as, with a giggle, Tania tripped on the first step of the back staircase.

'Sorry — still on a high. Haven't done this for years. I mean creeping up the back stairs.'

She thought she heard Luke mutter something that sounded like 'Not since Harry I suppose.' She turned, but he pushed her, not very gently, onwards and upwards. 'Hurry up before the night porter comes to find out what the racket's all about.' His hands came into contact with her jeans-clad backside as he gave her a hefty shove.

'Ever Sir Galahad,' she giggled before carrying on.

They padded down the first floor corridor. 'I'm in here.' Tania reached a door then turned to face him and waited. Under the leather jacket, Luke could see her chest rising and falling as she breathed lightly, excited, charged, and ready — for him.

He didn't know how he was going to do it, but he had to.

'I'm on the next floor,' he said quietly.

'Luke?' Her jewel eyes clouded with incomprehension.

'Early start in the morning. You can let me have the jacket and helmet back at breakfast. Sleep well.'

Tania blinked. He was gone. All that remained to remind her of their night ride were lingering smells of oil and the leather of their jackets.

8

Luke wasn't in the dining room the next morning. Tania had spent a sleepless night dreading this moment — and he wasn't here.

Ordering juice and black coffee, she glanced round the other tables. There was the usual scattering of tourists and businessmen reading newspapers. She tried to see if he was hiding behind one of the broadsheets but, instinctively, she knew that wasn't his way. If he had anything to say, he'd be totally upfront about it — and Tania had no doubt that they'd be exchanging words of some sort before the day was through.

Which was what had landed her in that most horribly embarrassing predicament last night. Why hadn't she kept quiet and not opened her big mouth? She could not believe she'd done anything so crass. She'd virtually offered herself on a plate — and he'd turned her down. She was still blushing all over as she remembered what had been the negative stroke to beat all negative strokes. She hadn't realised she was so out of practice. Luke had reminded her — and how! She'd have to resign from the commission. This time it wasn't open for negotiation.

The waiter delivered her coffee and Tania drank two cups without tasting a thing.

Where on earth was Luke?

There was movement in the doorway and Tania felt a sick feeling in the pit of her stomach. She knew, without looking up, that this was it. Luke strode into the dining room, blue eyes raking the tables until they lighted on her. Unaware of the flurry of female focus his entrance caused, he crossed the room in record time. He was one angry man. Tania tossed her head, annoyed at this inequality of the sexes. After all, she'd only turned the tables on him. He'd made a play for her the previous night

186

and she was damned if she'd wear sackcloth and ashes. Why should she?

'Finished?' he clipped at Tania. If he was aware of how many feminine pairs of eyes were surveying him hungrily from behind their tabloid newspapers, he didn't show it.

Neither was there any evidence of the bike-riding champion of the night before. He'd showered off the dirt and his jet-black hair was freshly washed. Tania couldn't help noticing how the ends curled over the collar of his sweatshirt. It gave her a funny feeling in the tip of her fingers. The dress was smart casual, but the body language was business.

'Er . . . yes.' Tania grabbed his jacket and helmet and thrust them at him. 'Here.'

'Leave those.'

'But . . . '

'We have to get to the house.'

'Why?' She was speaking to Luke's back. 'Not another break-in? What's happened?'

She caught up with him in the foyer.

'Stupid Shuna. That's what.' He tossed his key on to the desk. 'Oh, and by the way, there isn't a room for us here tonight.'

'What?'

'We'll sort it out later.'

Long as Tania's legs were, they were no match for Luke's as she found herself galloping after him again, out into the newborn May morning air. She wanted to linger and breathe in its beauty, but Luke's face was thunder as he eased himself into his car and Tania dismissed the thought as a bad idea. Luke had already started the Ferrari's engine and Tania was forced to scramble in beside him, her own heart beating faster than was humanly possible. Whatever it was that Shuna had done, Tania sent up a silent prayer of relief. It had let her off the hook.

Luke's scarlet monster of a car made the silent journey in moments. Tania plaited and replaited her fingers, a nervous reaction she thought she'd outgrown. This was terrible. She wasn't good at apologising, but she ought to do something soon to ease the atmosphere. Where on earth did she start? And what was she sorry for? Sorry she'd offered herself on a plate? Or sorry he'd turned her down?

'Luke,' she took a deep breath, 'About last night . . . '

'Forget it.' He swept in through the entrance gates.

'We have to talk.' Tania was on a roll and Luke wasn't going to stop her. Shuna's white car was still parked outside The Lodge. Luke was out of his own car in seconds, leaving Tania open-mouthed for a moment. Then she scurried along after him, yet again.

'What is going on?' she panted, losing patience. 'And will you stop treating me like some sort of concubine trailing after her lord and master?'

'Shuna?' Luke bellowed, still ignoring Tania. 'You upstairs?'

His voice echoed round the empty rooms. Muttering a curse that raised

Tania's eyebrows in appreciation of its originality, he turned on his heel.

'Come on.'

'Now where're we going?'

'There have been complaints from the neighbours about last night. The vicar's been on the blower. He's had half the parish bending his ear.'

'Surely not. I mean, we were only a few moments revving up . . . ' 'I'm not talking about the bike.'

'Then what?'

'That.' By this time they were halfway down the gravel drive to the house. Luke put his hands on Tania's shoulders and whisked her round to face the misty peacock lawn. There'd been heavy dew and the sunshine hadn't yet dried it out.

'Oh.' It was a long drawn out sigh of satisfaction and it came from Tania. 'How lovely.'

Through the gauzy haze, Tania caught flashes of green, deep blue and gold. A lump lodged in her throat as she remembered past May mornings and similar scenes, before Harry . . .

'Lovely be blowed.' Luke's voice scythed through her memories. The lawn was graced with a small pride of blue peacocks, several females over-shadowed by the flamboyant males and the stark white of one albino. 'They've been here all night, mournful and wailing loud enough to wake the dead.'

'But they're supposed to do that. You wouldn't understand.' Tania leapt to their defence.

'I understand better than you think,' Luke muttered under his breath. Hell, he thought to himself, he'd thought she was beautiful before, but now . . . His body tightened in masculine reaction.

Tania took a step forward. There was a rustling sound and one of the male peacocks fanned his tail feathers, vibrating them into a shimmering sea of turquoise, jade, and bronze and strutting round the lawn like a sun king.

'Where did they come from?'

Luke dragged himself back to the present.

'One of Shuna's friend's has a manor house or something. She had this hare-brained scheme,' his blue eyes narrowed in her direction. 'Or was it your idea?' He needed to feel angry with her. Blame her for this, even though he knew it wasn't her fault. If he didn't, he wouldn't be liable for the consequences.

Tania's smile of appreciation was washed away in a flash. 'My idea?'

'Stupid things have been interfering with the night watchman too. Poor sod got the fright of his life when they looked in the windows at him. Thought they were some sort of ghost.'

Tania couldn't stop a smile of appreciation crossing her face.

'At least they didn't break in through a window, because the locks had been changed, and frighten the wits out of him.'

'That wasn't my fault.'

'Neither is this mine.'

192

They glared at each other before Luke said, 'this isn't getting us anywhere. We'll have to shift them.'

'We? Why we? This is nothing to do with me.'

Tania recoiled from the lightning laser of Luke's eyes. 'Shuna said you told her about the peacocks . . . '

'I did, but I didn't expect her to charge off and get some.' Was he deliberately trying to inflame her?

'Well she did. Look at them.'

'Aren't they beautiful?' Tania couldn't be angry. 'Peacocks should be therapy,' she glanced at Luke out the corner of her eyes, 'for stressed out cyber kings, or whatever you call yourself.'

Luke glared down at her. Something in Tania's face softened the anger in his own eyes. 'They are beautiful,' he admitted reluctantly, 'but we can't keep them. Not yet. Anyway.'

'I suppose not,' Tania agreed, casting a lingering look in their direction. She wished she had a camera. This was something else to add to the list of things Ellie wouldn't believe. She had so much to tell her sister!

'What am I going to do?' There was none of the international financier about Luke now. It gladdened Tania's heart that, when it came to a domestic crisis, he panicked like everyone else. 'Help me. I'm open to suggestions.'

'We'll think of something,' she said with a confidence she was far from feeling.

'Atagirl!'

The blue of Luke's eyes deepened and he raised a hand to her face. His touch on her cheek sparked off another wave of memory deep inside Tania. She'd been down this route before. She was more than certain that, somewhere, her past had clashed with Luke's — but where? And when?

'Tania? About last night . . . I didn't mean to . . . Flattered, really . . . ' His hair was in need of a cut she noticed as he raked it with his fingers. She wished he wouldn't do that. It made him look vulnerable, an emotion she didn't want to associate with him.

'I'm sorry, Luke. I shouldn't have pushed it.' She felt foolish as she almost shouted her words, having to raise her voice above the wails of the peacocks as they seemed to be growing more agitated.

Luke raised his eyes. 'Whoever thought these things were romantic need their brains tested. They're doing unmentionable things to the lawn as well. I've just skidded on something very unpleasant.'

There was a loud screech of brakes. The builders' vans were arriving, one or two of the drivers swerving and cursing the elegant creatures who had decided to stroll into the path of their oncoming vehicles. Tania, all thoughts of romance flying out the window, laughed out loud at the sight of the peacocks side-stepping on to the gravel path like characters out of a cartoon film.

'What's going on guv?' the foreman called over.

'Can you get them into your van?'

Luke demanded.

'Do me a favour mate. There's bricks and stuff in the back.'

'That albino's highly-strung.' Tania gripped Luke's arm. 'Look at it.'

The bird in question was advancing menacingly on a hapless workman who was busy backing into his van.

Luke groaned and ran a hand through his dark hair making it stand on end. One of the males immediately raised its tail, displaying eye topped feather tips ringed with sapphire and gold, which fluttered to and fro as he began his courtship ritual. Tania giggled again.

'You're in luck.' She had difficulty getting the words out.

'Hmm?' Luke was peering into the back of the contractor's van.

'They do that thing with their feathers when they're mating. Think you're on to a winner, Luke! His sexuality's a bit doubtful though so I'd back against the nearest wall if I were you.'

The workman guffawed and Luke glared at her, banging his head on the roof of the van. There was another muffled oath. 'It's not funny. And that's two bumps you owe me.' He rubbed the top of his head as he spun round.

'Losing it Luke?' Tania was determined not to feel guilty, even if he did look a bit pale.

She preferred him this way — in a situation where she called the shots. It made him seem more human. Not strictly in control.

'Will you stop babbling on about sex and do something?'

'I don't see how I can help.' If Luke was going to blame her for this fiasco, Tania thought, she may as well get mileage out of it. 'I'm only the interior designer. Shuna got them here. She's your wife. Tell her to get them out.'

Luke raised both his hands in a gesture of menace and, for one second, Tania thought he was going to launch himself at the flirtatious peacock and strangle it. The builder did too.

'Steady on, mate. Don't lose your bottle. Look,' he pointed down the drive in relief, 'your lady friend's coming.'

Even the peacocks stopped wailing and jerked their plumed heads at the serious competition sauntering down the carriage drive. Today Shuna was wearing purple pants and a pink top. With her sun-tanned skin and shiny cap of dark hair, she cast even the peacock into the shade.

'Bloody 'ell,' said the foreman.

Tania couldn't have put it better herself.

'Hello Luke.' She ignored Tania. 'Where were you last night? I wanted to show you my present. Do you like them?'

'You brainless, id . . . '

'Luke,' Tania snapped.

'Stay out of this.'

There was more activity on the lawn and a rustling of tail feathers.

'You're frightening the peacocks.'

'Get them out of here. Now.' Luke

seemed to be the only male on the premises not blinded by Shuna's brilliance. The workmen were still standing around gaping at the scene unfolding in front of their eyes. The peacocks too were temporarily stilled, Tania noticed.

Shuna's almond eyes darkened nastily. 'Tania said you wanted things done your way. She said you wanted peacocks here. Isn't that right, Tania?'

A furnace of flame flared inside Tania. She was sick of playing fall guy between these two.

'Get your own lives sorted out,' she snapped. 'I'm going upstairs to get on with my work. I presume you want me to go ahead, Luke? As we discussed last night?' If Luke wouldn't listen to her, she wasn't going to resign. Besides she'd done a rethink on that one. 'You remember? Before you took me for a starlight spin on your Sportster?'

Tania felt quite pleased with her poetic description of their night ride. She had expected a reaction — from

Luke. She hadn't expected Shuna to become hysterical.

'The Sportster? You told me that you'd sold the bike!' In her agitation, her accent reverted to the Oriental of her youth. 'Where have you been hiding it?'

The look Luke threw at Tania almost pulled the teeth out of her head! Now what had she done? She decided not to stay around to find out.

'I'll be upstairs if you need me.'

She didn't look back as she hurried indoors. Already several voices were raised in altercation. She didn't know what had got them going, but she didn't want any part of it.

As she worked, she heard a cacophony of noises outside — vehicles on the gravel, more raised voices, peacocks wailing, and the rushing of tail feathers — and then silence. More than once she was tempted to look out of the window but, with monumental self-control she carried on working. As usually happened when she was engaged in a project she loved, she didn't notice the hours pass and it was only her stomach which eventually let her know it had been a long time since her breakfast of orange juice.

The sunlight was slanting its afternoon angle across the veranda and Tania realised it had been quiet outside for quite a while. Perhaps it was safe to look out. She stood on tiptoe and craned her neck to see what, if anything, was happening on the lawn.

'We'll have to stay in The Lodge tonight.'

Tania didn't know if it was the shock of what Luke had said, or his sudden appearance from nowhere, that dried her mouth. She cannoned against his chest as she jerked round. There was the familiar smell of earth and the great outdoors. Both quickened her heartbeat.

'The peacocks have gone,' he said, his breath tickling her ear. 'But they'll be back one day, when things are more settled. The builders have gone too.

They'll be back tomorrow.' He steadied her body, his hand clutching her arm. 'So, for this evening that just leaves you and me . . . '

'I'm not staying with you . . . '

'I've collected our stuff from The Feathers. Yours was all packed and ready, so I just brought it back here.'

'You've got a nerve.'

'The Feathers is fully booked.'

'Then I'll book somewhere else.'

'Everywhere is full. Shuna's friends are having some sort of summer bash. All the media wannabes are going. She's been invited, so she won't be bothering us tonight.'

'What about you?'

Tania couldn't imagine any serious hostess not including Luke on her list.

'I'm not going.'

'Why not?'

'Can't stand those sort of functions. Besides, the invitation didn't include you.'

Tania felt as though the shaky veranda had collapsed under her feet.

'That was quite a body blow,' she gave a half-laugh. 'For a moment there I believed you.'

'I'm not joking.'

One look at the intensity in Luke's blue eyes was enough to convince Tania. He was speaking the truth.

'We're not joined at the hip and we're certainly not an item.'

'We've some unfinished business to discuss,' he said in the slowest, sexiest voice Tania had ever heard from a man.

What on earth was she going to do now? If everywhere was fully booked, there was nothing for it but to drive back to town. She didn't relish the idea, but it was the only advisable option. It had the bonus, too, of putting as many miles as possible between herself and Luke.

'Come on,' Luke said. 'We're finished for the day here. I've got us some langoustines and white wine. Let's have a party of our own.'

Every instinct screamed at Tania to refuse his offer. Which was why two hours later, showered and changed into a silk shift dress, she was sitting opposite Luke in the tiny kitchen of The Lodge, licking garlic butter off her fingers and dipping langoustines into a sauce straight from heaven. Outside, the early evening sun danced on the postage stamp lawn and, in the far distance, they could hear strains of music from Shuna's friends' party.

'She won't be back,' Luke paused. 'Ever.'

'It doesn't matter.'

'Why not?' There was a quickening glint in Luke's eyes.

'When I first met you . . . ' Tania frowned as Luke jerked involuntarily. 'What is it?'

'When we first met?' His voice sounded a bit shaky.

'On the bridge . . . ' Tania paused. There was an expression she didn't understand on Luke's face. 'Luke?'

'Go on,' he urged, through tightened jaw muscles.

'I didn't want this job. I was trying to

think of ways of getting out of it. Then I saw the house . . . '

He relaxed, 'And it worked its magic on you.'

'It's still no commitment, Luke. You were the one to lay down the ground rules.'

'How about a renegotiation of terms?'

'I'm serious, Luke, even if you aren't. No relationship.'

Luke went for her jugular. 'Those weren't the vibes you were giving out last night.'

Flames leapt up Tania's face, scorching her skin at the memory. 'I was going to resign this morning. That's why my things were packed.'

'The hell you were.' There was an angry scar running from Luke's cheek down the side of his face. It whitened with his anger. 'I'll decide when your job here is finished. And, as for last night,' he took a slow swallow of wine, the blue eyes never leaving hers, 'the timing wasn't right.'

'Timing?'

'You ought to be grateful to Shuna. She's done us a favour.'

'Luke, I'm going.' If he came on heavy, she knew she hadn't the will to resist.

'You're not going anywhere. You've demolished a good half of this excellent Frascati.'

'The walk to The Feathers will clear my head. I can get the car and be in . . .'

'I still have your keys. Remember?' He gave a low laugh as Tania cursed. She'd completely forgotten he hadn't given them back to her. 'You see, there's nothing I haven't thought of.'

Tania began to panic as control of the situation slipped from her fingers. Luke was serious. He was going to seduce her. He'd planned the whole thing down to the last detail. And the real horror of the situation was that she didn't want to stop him!

Thoroughly unsettled by the intimacy of the smile touching Luke's mouth, Tania could only stare at him. The light was beginning to fade from the day. In the smoky dusk of the evening, she could feel her control of reality slipping from her grasp. She'd never wanted anything in her life as much as she wanted Luke Sinclair to make love to her here, now, if necessary, on the floor of the kitchen. Her wantonness appalled her. She must have heatstroke. There was no other logical explanation.

'I don't know what you're talking about.' She had to fight for her sanity.

'I know your senses were dulled by salmon and blackberry tart, but you must remember our first dinner at The Feathers and our little conversation about peacocks.' Tania didn't think it was possible for her body clock to tick any faster.

'After today,' she felt as though her tonsils were lined with sandpaper, 'I'd have thought peacocks were the last thing you'd want to talk about.'

'Your nose was all red from too much

sun,' Luke continued ruthlessly, 'and your hair was doing its usual fight for independence thing, curls bouncing all over the place.' He touched a stray curl at the side of her face, 'Just like it is now. Lets you down every time, doesn't it? That's why I want to make love to you, and why I refused last night. Remember when I made the first offer? What you said?' Tania closed her eyes. Dear Lord. What had she said? 'You said it would be a 'No' until the peacocks returned to The Peacock House.'

'Luke,' she gritted her teeth. 'No.'

'The peacocks came back today. I take that as a green light. Wouldn't you?'

'Don't.'

'What's the matter? Don't you like me touching you?' His next question was dark as treacle. 'Or do you like it too much? Is all this 'I am my own woman' thing just a big act?'

'Stop it.'

He let the curl fall from his fingers

and Tania wanted to howl with dismay.

'As you wish.'

She didn't quite know how it happened, but Luke was on his feet and dragging her from her chair and kissing her before she'd had time to realise the rock solid wall against her body was his chest.

'Still don't remember? Our first meal at The Feathers?'

Tania was past remembering anything now. 'Luke.' She was past recognising that the dreadful groaning noise she could hear was her own voice saying his name.

There was a swish and her dress formed a silk circle round her feet. It was followed seconds later by her underwear, then Luke's clothes. Their bodies were so hot, their skin clung against each other's. Through a mist of moisture, Tania felt the briefest pain as Luke lowered her to the floor then entered her with rhythmic thrusts that grew more urgent with their equally increasing demands.

Fireworks from the party lit the night sky as Tania climaxed in unison with Luke who groaned his release against her chest as his body slipped from hers.

Round them, on the floor, lay scattered fragments of langoustine shells, spilt wine, and garlic butter. The mess should have made Tania shudder. It didn't. She'd never felt so blissfully happy in her life.

'We can't stay here,' she vaguely heard Luke's voice as he lifted her into his arms as easily as if she were as petite as Ellie and not five-foot-ten in her stockinged feet. 'Phew,' he made a noise of disgust, 'we both smell like a fish market on a bad day.' His voice coated Tania in love and laughter as he carried her upstairs. Through the open windows, she could have sworn she heard the mournful wail of another peacock.

With a sigh she collapsed on to the bed, Luke on top of her. Within moments, she was asleep.

9

Tania overslept again the next morning.

Luke's side of the bed was cold and empty when she woke up. She rolled over on her side, luxuriating in the cocooning comfort before she remembered. She threw back the sheets and looked down at her body. There was no outward evidence of the previous night's activities, apart from a slight bruise staining the top of her left thigh. Tania stroked it, welcoming its tenderness, then felt a flutter of sickness as the physical details of her intimacies with Luke returned to haunt her with full power.

Dear Lord, had she really let him make love to her on the kitchen floor amidst the remains of their meal? Had they woken in the night, showered together, and made love again? Had he really whispered in her ear that he loved her?

Yes. Yes. Yes.

The answer to all three questions was positive. Tania put a hand to her forehead. It was as hot as a furnace. She saw in the bedroom mirror her eyes, too, were deep pools of hot aquamarine — if such a thing existed. What had possessed her? Temporary madness. There was no other explanation. She'd never done anything so insane in her life before. Until a few weeks ago, she'd been on the fast track to terminal spinsterhood. If Ellie hadn't pushed her into this job, she'd still be there. Everything evolved back to Ellie. Tania bit her lip. It wasn't fair to blame her sister. Tania was a fully mature adult, responsible for her own life and capable of making her own decisions. And *what* a decision she'd made last night! If that didn't beat all, then there was no justice. She shivered again as she remembered the moments of intimacy, the whispered endearments, the masculine smell of Luke's body, and the roughness of male flesh on hers. It had been a long time since she'd been down that road. Of course, she'd had boyfriends in the past, not that many, but enough to let her know the physical act of making love wasn't all it was supposed to be. Nothing had happened to shake her from her belief — until last night. A tremor ran through her body as she remembered the dangerous flash of blue eyes, the jet-black hair, the brooding sexual awareness. Clearly a formula when combined with *her* genes, that was more explosive than dynamite.

Luke. Her stomach did a quick tango. What had made her take a U-turn so decisively?

It had to be the peacocks. They'd always been a catalyst for her emotions. She'd fallen in love — or thought she had — with Harry, as the peacocks strutted their stuff on the lawn. And yesterday, they'd worked their charm on her again. Nothing would happen between her and Luke until the peacocks returned. That was what Luke had said. And his words had unerringly come true.

She should be feeling euphoric. But why did she have this feeling of unease? Like a puppet being worked by emotions she couldn't control. Where was Luke now? She had to find him. Tania snatched up a robe and tightened it round her body. Movement triggered her appetite. She felt ravenous. Perhaps Luke had put some coffee on to percolate.

'Luke?' She padded down the stairs. No reply. The kitchen was empty. Tania was almost too embarrassed to look at the floor, but it had been cleaned. There was no trace of the previous night's debauchery. Only a faint tang of garlic lingered on the air.

But where was Luke? she asked herself again, trying to ignore the bolt of apprehension weighing down her stomach. He'd just gone up to the house, that was all. Nothing to worry about, she tried to convince herself.

She'd get some coffee on the go, shower and then go up there herself. She bustled round the kitchen, opening the back door to let in the sunshine and rid the air of the redolent smell of garlic.

It took Tania a few moments to realise the faint ringing in her ears was actually her mobile telephone, and a few more seconds to locate her bag.

'Luke?' She switched on, gasping his name in relief. 'Where are you?' There was a moment's silence.

'Tania?'

'Ellie.' Overcome with embarrassment, Tania sank on to a wooden kitchen chair. Now she'd well and truly done it. Her sister would be on to the scent of intrigue faster than any bloodhound.

'Where are you? I've been trying the studio and your mobile for ages.'

'Still in Lower Chipping.' Tania glanced at her mobile. There were umpteen text messages — unread.

'And you were supposed to be coming down to visit me. I've sent the boys and Charles to his mother. It's been an age since I've seen you.'

The invitation had completely slipped Tania's mind. 'Sorry darling. I've been so busy. We'll catch up later.'

Ellie wasn't going to be got rid of that easily. 'Busy with Luke Sinclair, I suppose. You're a fast worker! There was I, despairing of you ever finding a man, dreading having an old maid for a sister. Virtually having to keel haul you to even meet Luke Sinclair, and now I can't entice you away from him. What is going on? Last I heard from you, he was Little Chipping's answer to the Grim Reaper. Now when I phone you up, you're breathing his name down the telephone as if . . . '

'For heaven's sake, Ellie, our relationship is professional.' Which wasn't strictly a lie. It was professional — and personal . . . deeply personal. Tania was glad Ellie couldn't see her sister rapidly turning tomato red.

'You mean there's nothing going on between the two of you?' Ellie didn't sound in the least convinced.

Tania knew it would be impossible to fool her sister. She could smell a subterfuge at fifty paces, but she gave it a go.

'It's not what you think.'

'No?'

Tania's heart dipped to her stomach. Her instincts had been right. She hadn't fooled Ellie.

'I have been busy.'

'I'm sure you have and you've told me that once already.'

Tania tucked her hair behind her ear, wondering how long it would take to get rid of Ellie. There were a million things she should be doing instead of justifying herself to a nosy sister who had nothing better to do than sit around all day and gossip.

'Listen Ellie, lovely talking to you and all that . . .'

'Tell me — did Luke spend the night with you?' The question cracked down the line, forthright in its bluntness even by Ellie's standards.

'Ellie. Please.' The bathrobe was too warm, reminding Tania that she wanted a shower. She wrinkled her nose. It also had a very unsettling scent of jasmine about it.

'Not being nosy, Tania, honest. Only I've lots to tell you. I hope you haven't . . . well . . . you know . . . done it . . . with Luke . . . or anything like that.'

'Anything like what?' Tania decided it was time to be firm with Ellie. They told each other most things, but there were limits to their sisterly intimacies. And Ellie had just crossed the threshold of Tania's tolerance.

'There's something you ought to know.'

'When I need you to run my life Ellie, I'll ask. Now I have to ring off. I've loads to do. I'll try to visit next weekend.' She didn't like arguing with Ellie, so she softened the blow a bit, 'The sooner I can get on, the sooner I'll be with you.'

'No, Tania, don't go. I really do have something to tell you — something mega-important. About Luke.'

'What's that?' Tania had only been paying half-attention as she hunted round for the jug kettle. If she didn't have some coffee soon, she'd die. Perhaps Ellie would get the message that this conversation was over if she banged a few cupboard doors.

'I can't tell you down the line. These things aren't safe.'

Tania looked round in desperation. Where was the kettle? 'What?'

'People listen in or something. You know like . . . '

'Ellie, I haven't a clue what you're talking about, but if I don't get my shot of caffeine within the next ten minutes . . . '

'I've found out some very interesting things about Luke Sinclair.' Tania tried to listen, then stiffened. There was a noise outside, a car door, then footsteps. Luke was back.

'Things you ought to know.' Ellie was babbling on, unaware she'd lost her audience. Tania was busy trying to tidy the tangle of her hair and wishing she didn't look quite so wanton in her borrowed bathrobe. Her face, too, was a dead give-away with its telltale flush of recent sex. The look was unmistakable, even to Tania's inexperienced eyes.

'You remember I told you Charles was getting nowhere trying to find out about him? The business is pukka and all that, but his personal life was a closed book. I know he was in the glossies when he married Shuna S but, before that, it was a blank book. Charles said he couldn't find out anything. How pathetic can you get?'

'Ellie, really not now, love.'

'Men are hopeless at that sort of thing anyway.' It was as if Tania hadn't spoken. 'Well I had a go. And you'll never believe it . . . '

'I'll call you back soon.'

Someone was coming through the front door.

'What the . . . ?' Tania cut Ellie off.

Her breath stabbed her in the chest as she realised she'd made the most ghastly mistake. She didn't need to turn round to know it wasn't Luke standing behind her. She would have recognised that smell of jasmine anywhere.

'What the hell are you doing here wearing my robe?'

There was a screech and, the next moment, Tania found herself flat on the floor with Shuna on top of her doing her best to scratch out her eyes.

'You've spent the night with my husband. Here. In my bed.'

They rolled round the floor like two brawling urchins. Tania felt her head crack on the table leg. It was her turn to lash out. She got Shuna squarely on the shin with a lightning rabbit punch. When it came to physical fitness, Shuna was no match for Tania. With her heavier weight and equally boiling outrage she was able, with another well-aimed kick, to flatten Shuna and leap to her feet before the smaller girl had time to get her wind.

'For heaven's sake, calm down, Shuna.'

'Don't you tell me to calm down, you cow.'

There was nothing of the elegant sophisticate about Shuna now. She was a primitive woman displaying all the naked emotions of her sex.

'If it makes you feel any better, I'm sorry that I borrowed your robe. I didn't know it was yours.' Tania tried her best to defuse the situation but Shuna was having none of it.

'I know all about you and Luke. Luke told me.'

There was ice instead of blood flowing through Tania's veins. The knock she'd just received on her head was nothing to the verbal slap in the face Shuna had just delivered.

'What did you say?'

Shuna staggered into a chair. Tania longed to shake the girl to see if her hair ever moved. Every strand was still in place, whereas she resembled the wild man of Borneo. It was Tania's face that was now Neolithic with rage. What on earth was going on here?

There was a triumphant little smile on Shuna's lips.

'He didn't tell you?'

'Tell me what?' Tania clamped her arms to her side, not daring to move. She was so angry, she was scared what she might do if she moved.

'We had a stupid row last night. A tiff.'

'Luke . . . '

'I'm not feeling well at the moment. My hormones are all over the place.'

There was a malicious smile on Shuna's face, and Tania had the feeling she wasn't going to like what she was going to hear. She could tell Shuna wasn't about to let her off lightly.

'I was annoyed with Luke, so I went to my friends' party on my own.' The expression on the other woman's face reminded Tania of a cat licking a bowl of cream. 'Luke had some chivalrous idea about taking you, but I told him that employees weren't invited. Besides, it was friends and close family only — and you don't fall into either group.'

Tania refused to be riled. Shuna was nothing more than a spiteful kitten testing her claws.

'Luke told me you'd gone for good.'

Shuna gave her irritating little laugh. 'He was mad at me, that's all. That's why he went with you. He couldn't take you to the party to make me jealous, so he had a party here — with you. Then, because I hadn't seen you together, he came to tell me all about it. How else would I know you've been here all night and that you had langoustines in garlic butter?'

Tania's palms itched to slap Shuna's beautifully made-up face. She didn't want to believe her but her words held a hollow ring of truth.

A bright shaft of sunlight cut through the window and Tania noticed with malicious pleasure the dark circles under Shuna's eyes that no make-up in the world could disguise.

'It was an all-night party. Did you know?'

Tania shook her head. She couldn't

remember how long the music had gone on for. She and Luke had had other things on their minds. She seemed to remember fireworks at some stage, but they could have been between herself and Luke. Nothing seemed real any more. Or made much sense.

'We had breakfast together.'

'We?'

'Luke and I. Down by the lake. It was beautifully cool. We watched the sun birthing . . .'

Hysteria twisted Tania's lips. What kind of new age speak was that? She wanted to laugh out loud, but she was scared that it would sound like a howl of outrage.

'Scrambled eggs, smoked salmon, and champagne.'

'Luke's been here with me.'

'I know. But where is he now?' Shuna couldn't keep the triumph out of her voice. Tania clutched the table — Shuna had a point. Where was Luke?

'I didn't have any champagne.' Shuna

laid a delicate hand on her flat stomach. 'I can't drink at the moment.'

'You didn't have any smoked salmon either. The whole thing's a pack of lies from start to finish. What did you say?' Tania's eyes were suddenly riveted to the tiny hand covering the silk front of her dress.

'I'm expecting a baby, Tania. I came back to tell Luke. It's just been confirmed. We had Easter together in Cannes and we stayed on a friend's yacht. Luke's so happy and so am I.'

A red mist formed behind Tania's eyes. Luke Sinclair had truly played her for a sucker. He'd known about Shuna's baby yet, because of a silly argument between them, he used her to get back at Shuna. How could she have been so blind? All that nonsense about the peacocks was just a ruse. She'd known from day one that Luke was still madly in love with his ex-wife. And hadn't he said that he wasn't looking for a relationship — permanent or otherwise? He couldn't have spelled it out more clearly.

'I can understand how angry you must be, Tania. A woman of your age doesn't want to be without a man. I'm sorry to have to break the news to you, really I am. Luke's like me — heartless, ambitious, and selfish. We're two of a kind.'

Tania didn't want to hear any more. She couldn't believe what she'd done. She'd broken every professional rule in her book, and one moment of madness had wiped out her career's integrity.

'You ran off with that singer — Xavier. It was in all the glossies. The baby could be his.'

'It's not,' Shuna said with an angry frown.

'You only came back because he ditched you.'

Tania couldn't believe what she'd just said. She'd always prided herself on personal dignity. Mud slinging had never been her style — until now. She wanted to lash out, to hurt someone.

Shuna was the only available target.

A shadow crossed Shuna's face, then she shrugged. 'These things happen in our world. They mean nothing and Luke understands. He understands everything about me. But the baby is his. Xavier's been touring for the past two months, so . . . ' She graced Tania with a sickly sweet smile, 'Even you can work it out. And I'm not lying — about anything.'

Tania didn't want to believe Shuna but, deep down, she knew that she spoke the truth. She was still wearing her strappy scarlet creation that screamed designer and tiny gold sandals that would have cost all the hefty commission Tania had intended slamming on Luke. And Shuna did look like she'd been up all night. And if she and Luke had watched the sun break through the early morning mist . . . Tania's throat locked.

'I see,' was the best she could manage. Her vocal chords were in danger of seizing up.

'So,' Shuna tucked her slim legs round the chair leg, 'where does that leave us?'

Tania pulled herself together. She may have made a fool of herself, but no one could call her a wimp. 'I came here to do a job. Mr Sinclair hired me . . . '

'He was too embarrassed to tell you this himself.'

'Tell me what?'

'He's going back to America today — some sort of crisis to do with one of the partners. He has to be there. He asked me to tell you . . . '

Tania's mobile rang again. She snatched it up. Any interruption was welcome. 'Hello?'

'Tania? Luke.'

Any interruption except this, Tania thought, turning her back on Shuna. Whatever it was he had to say, she couldn't face his wife.

'Where are you?'

'On the way to Heathrow. Look, I'm sorry to desert you like this, but something's cropped up. I have to get back to the States. Can you manage without me for a while?'

'I can manage without you forever,' Tania heard herself say as she flicked the end button, biting down the bile rising in her throat. Leaving herself no room to rethink, she turned back to Shuna. 'And I can manage without you too.'

'That was Luke wasn't it?' Shuna didn't look quite so confident.

'Yes.'

'Then you're going?' There was an eager little smile on Shuna's lips.

'I'm staying to finish the job,' Tania said firmly.

'Have you no pride? Luke won't want you around . . .'

'A job is a job. I gave up everything to take on this commission and I'm not walking out on it now. Luke Sinclair owes me. Now are you getting out — or do I have to throw you out?'

Shuna jumped to her feet. 'It's not your place to throw me out.'

Then, with one look at the light of murder in Tania's eyes, she turned swiftly, her heels clip clopping on the floor as she fled The Lodge.

10

Luke's flight landed back at Heathrow in the early evening. With minimal luggage, he was quickly through Customs and Excise. His driver was waiting in the Executive car park.

'Good trip, sir?'

Luke flung his briefcase on to the back seat. It had been a really awful trip, a complete waste of time. He hadn't slept for forty-eight hours, and all for nothing.

'Yes. Thank you,' he answered automatically. He was unfailingly polite to his employees, but he hoped his driver wasn't in a chatty mood as today might be the day he broke his rule of natural courtesy.

'Where to sir?'

Luke hesitated before saying, 'Little Chipping,' hoping against hope that Tania was there. It was a long shot. If she wasn't, he'd scour every corner of the country until he found her. There'd been no reply from her London flat or her mobile. He'd got a secretary from the New York office to keep ringing regularly and report back to him — without success. Things weren't looking good — she'd gone to ground. Luke's body tightened. There was nowhere she could escape him.

The car negotiated the airport tunnel and complex exits and was soon heading west on the M4. Luke closed his eyes. He had meant to sleep, but his brain wouldn't let him. He was too wired up to relax. He hadn't been able to sleep on the flight either. Where was Tania? He hadn't a clue. And what on earth had she meant about carrying on without him forever? What had happened? He smelt Shuna's mischief somewhere. She'd told him she was going back to France when he'd bumped into her outside The Lodge after buying the langoustines and the champagne. He also thought he'd caught sight of her as he'd left The Lodge the next morning. At the time, he'd thought it had been a trick of the light. But what if she hadn't gone back? What if she and those friends of hers had been making trouble?

When it came to scruples, Shuna didn't have any. Why had he ever got tangled up with her in the first place? The questions bounced backwards and forwards. But no matter how many times he asked them, he couldn't find a sensible explanation for Tania's disappearance. Shuna had known he was going back to the States, but she hadn't known the visit had been brought forward — unless it really had been her outside that morning, spying on him. Anything was possible.

If only that telephone call hadn't come just as he'd been getting dressed. He'd planned breakfast with Tania outside on the tiny patio, and then . . .

His lips twisted in a grimace. Heaven help him, he'd been going to propose to her. Laid-back was supposed to have been the name of his game. He'd meant every word when he'd originally told Tania he wasn't looking for a relationship but when those eyes had flashed at him with such fire, he was instantly transported back ten years, when he'd been hopelessly in love with her and she hadn't even realised he'd existed. No, he didn't want anything as casual as a relationship. He wanted marriage.

The sapphire ring still nestled on its bed of velvet in a box in Luke's pocket. He'd go down on one knee in front of the entire population of Little Chipping if she'd just say 'Yes'. He hadn't meant to move forward so quickly, but Shuna producing those blasted peacocks, and then Tania coming on so heavily that night at The Feathers . . . it had all been too much for him. And now it looked like he'd blown the whole thing!

He'd waited so long, been so careful not to rock the boat. In the ten years since Harry had died, there hadn't been one day when he hadn't thought of Tania. The leggy teenager in the fruit patch had grown into the most desirable woman he had ever known. He felt masculine warmth in his loins. She'd been beautiful at eighteen — now she was a knockout.

He'd worshipped her from afar, knowing he was no competition for Harry Fitzroy. He was the gardener's stepson, the boy with attitude who'd raced round the countryside on his motorbike full of angst — the boy who didn't even exist in Tania's life. Then Harry had died in that awful crash. Luke had gone over that time and again in his head. It hadn't been his fault. But local gossip hadn't seen it that way. He'd been the local bad boy with a reputation and he hadn't stood a chance. Tania had been packed off to London, and Luke had gone to America and met Shuna. She was as different from Tania as it was possible to be. Perhaps it was that which had attracted him to her. He'd wanted to forget Tania, forget Harry, forget the accident had ever happened. But he couldn't. And now ten years on, they were back to square one. He was still head-over-heels in love with her and she never wanted to see him again. Pain lanced his chest. Why? Had someone told her their distorted version of the truth of that terrible night? He felt as though he'd been punched in the stomach. Who? It couldn't have been Shuna. He'd never mentioned it to her. He'd never mentioned it to anyone. It wasn't a part of his life he was proud of, or wanted to remember. He'd moved on since those days, but the scars hadn't completely healed. They wouldn't until Tania . . . He mustn't go down that route. He had to find her first.

Why hadn't he left her a note before he left? It had been sheer lunacy not to. He'd wanted to, but he was scared he'd go over the top, tell her he loved her, that he couldn't live without her, that she had to promise to marry him. Coward that he was, he hadn't done it. He'd got that one well and truly wrong too. She must have woken up, found The Lodge empty, and thought he'd deserted her. What a prize idiot he'd been. He felt a stiffening in his body as he imagined the expression on Tania's face when she realised he'd gone. He hadn't meant to hurt her but, unsure how she'd react to his feelings, he hadn't put them to the test.

But why wouldn't she talk to him? He'd tried ringing her back immediately, but there'd been no answer on her mobile and then they'd called his flight.

Rain slapped the side of the car window. Luke flinched.

'Been like this for two days now, sir,' the driver looked into his mirror. 'More flooding, I shouldn't be surprised, makes the roads greasy and all. Like driving on ice.'

'Hmm.' Luke made a noise at the back of his throat. The driver's eyes flickered from the mirror back to the road.

Luke glanced at his watch. They should make Little Chipping by nine o'clock. He'd no idea what to expect, but it was a base to start from. He had to see Tania. Explain — what? That he hadn't wanted to wake her that morning, because she'd looked so gut-wrenchingly beautiful in sleep with that wonderful hair all over the pillow? So he'd slipped out quietly and telephoned her the first chance he'd got? Of course, he could see now it had been a really stupid thing to do. But if he'd wakened her, he wouldn't have been able to resist making love to her again. If only Hal hadn't made it sound like a full-scale emergency in the States, he'd have told him to sort the mess out himself. But he couldn't do that — not to his oldest colleague. He'd played the Good Samaritan to the hilt. Poor old Hal was losing it after his illness. Luke had had to fly out, and now Tania had walked out on him. Luke clenched his fists. He'd get her back if it meant dragging her all the way from wherever she was, by every curl of that stunning chestnut hair. He'd show her she couldn't walk out on him and get away with it.

'Feeling all right, sir?'

The driver's eyes were on the mirror again and Luke realised he'd groaned out loud.

'Sorry. Bit tired.'

'Jet-lag, I shouldn't be surprised.' The driver sounded reassured.

Luke wanted to shout at him to shut up. How on earth did he know what he was talking about? He'd crossed the Atlantic more times than the man had had hot dinners.

Instead he'd demanded, 'Can't you go any faster?'

'Not advisable in this weather, sir. Spray's something awful. Want to get there safely, don't we?'

Luke lapsed into silence again, his brain raging. He still hadn't told Tania who he was or what had really happened the night Harry had died. He'd wanted to get a ring firmly on her finger before he did. Ellie had only been eleven, so she couldn't have told Tania anything. It had been obvious from her body language at the dinner party when he'd first met her that she knew absolutely nothing about it. There was no way Tania could have found out what had happened the night Harry had died. Harry had been a mad lunatic driver, always speeding, but Luke had tried to look after him and he certainly hadn't been responsible for the drink Harry had consumed before the collision. But the locals hadn't seen it like that. They'd known Luke and his biker friends had been in the bar as well that night. Luke's lips twisted. The old feudal system was still rife in that backwater village. And ten years ago, Little Chipping had been the backwater to beat all backwaters. There was no way young Harry could be responsible for what had happened they'd said. They'd even covered up that business with Patti Saunders. And then there'd been his mother and stepfather to think of. They'd still have to live with the shame and the silent finger pointing.

That's why he'd cleared off to America the first chance he'd had. He couldn't beat their prejudices, so he'd left them to it.

Torturing himself with memories, Luke closed his eyes to the lull of the car as the tyres hissed over the wet roads. He desperately wanted to get some sleep. It was going to be a long night. At last his head fell forward.

'We're here, sir.'

Luke was awake in an instant and out of the car within seconds, the smell of damp earth clearing his head of sleep.

'Thanks. Book yourself a room at The Feathers for the night then take the car back to London. Sorry I was a bit abrupt.' He clapped the man on the shoulder, 'Nothing personal.'

'Right, sir. Thanks.' The driver pocketed the generous tip Luke handed him, then reversed the car round the flowerbed and drove slowly down the gravel drive.

There were no lights on in The Lodge, or cars on the forecourt. Luke

opened the door, smelt the emptiness of
The Lodge, threw his suitcases in and,
changing into his leathers in ten
seconds, slammed the door shut. There
was nothing for him here.

'Who's there?'

Luke flinched, temporarily blinded
by a torch searching the grounds.

'Put that thing out.'

'Oh, it's you, sir. Sorry. Saw the car
drive up. Wasn't expecting you.' The
security guard lowered his beam.
'Fancy some tea? I've just put a brew
on.'

'What's been happening?' Luke
asked, sipping tea from a mug and
perching on an upturned orange box in
the guard's makeshift den.

'Not a lot. The builders are doing
well. Been no more break-ins. The
visitors have all gone . . . '

'Visitors?' Luke stiffened.

'The ladies. Your wife . . . '

'My ex-wife.'

'Sorry sir. Keep forgetting. She's
been around so much, seems like you're

still married. You're getting back together, I hear?'

Luke crashed his mug down on the box. It swayed alarmingly under the impact. 'Whoever's putting round these rumours is out-of-line. Make sure everyone gets the message.'

'Right sir,' the guard hastily assured him, glancing uneasily around for his torch. He didn't like the look in Mr Sinclair's eyes at all. Funny lot these high-powered people. Could turn nasty, too, at the drop of a hat.

'She's gone anyway, back to France I think. So's the other lady — gone too. The designer one.'

'Miss Jordan?'

'That's the one. Went off in a bit of a hurry same day you . . . '

'Do you know where?'

'Can't say that I do.' The guard rubbed an ear. So that was the lie of the land? No wonder they'd all hared off quicker than rats up a drainpipe. Bit of hanky-panky likely as not.

Luke stood up. 'Thanks for the tea.'

'It's a filthy night, sir. You're not going out in this?'

Luke already had the door open, letting in a swirl of wind and rain. 'If Miss Jordan should come back . . . '

'Yes sir?' The guard prompted into the silence that had fallen between them.

'Tell her . . . ' The guard frowned. It didn't sound like the same man speaking. He wasn't given to flights of fancy, but he was certain there was a catch or lump, or something, distorting Luke Sinclair's voice. The man was under serious stress. The guard cleared his throat uneasily, wishing his wife were here. She was always good when things got emotional.

'Yes sir?' he prompted again, wishing he hadn't noticed Luke's eyes were glazed with emotion. That ex-wife of his was always acting a bit strange, now he came to think of it.

'Tell her I've been here looking for her.'

The guard raised his eyebrows

— hardly a message to get uptight about.

'Right. I'll do that. Er, where will you be?'

'London — at my Camden address.'

There was another blast of wet cold air as Luke disappeared into the night. The guard breathed a sigh of relief and poured himself some more tea.

Hunching his shoulders against the rain that had turned seriously unpleasant, Luke trudged down the drive. He welcomed the sharpness of the wet needles on his face. It gave him a reason to feel bad. He wanted to suffer physically. But no matter how hard he walked, he couldn't get Tania's face out of his mind. What had happened, he asked himself for he didn't know how many times? He wouldn't ring her London number again. If she were there, he'd surprise her. And she'd better not be with another man! He snarled into the rain. If there was someone else, they'd be on a short life expectancy.

In the distance, the welcoming lights of The Feathers were distorted by the wind and rain. Luke quickened his step — at last. The Harley should make the journey back to London in three hours or so. There shouldn't be too much traffic. Only a fool would go out on a night like this, he thought grimly.

'Hello sir,' the barman greeted him, 'Raining is it?' he asked with a cheerful smile as Luke dripped into the visitors' lounge.

Luke nodded. 'Come to collect the bike. Got the keys?'

The barman stopped polishing the glasses and began searching around under the bar. 'Here. Keys, but no bike.'

'What?' Luke snapped.

'If you'd like to wait till I close up, I'll run you over to your mother's. It's back in her garage. Thought you were going to be away for a while and, what with the model lady being around, well, such a valuable piece of machinery. You always said I was to . . . ' Luke collapsed on to a bar stool and ran his hands through his hair. Fate was against him at every turn. The barman took pity on his haunted face. He liked Luke Sinclair. He'd been a tearaway in his youth, according to rumour, but many lads went through that phase. It was a part of growing up. And he'd never believed all that nonsense about him and Harry Fitzroy. 'If it's really important, I'll see if I can get cover.'

★ ★ ★

'You look like a drowned rat, Luke,' his mother chided. 'And what time of night is this to come calling? It's nearly eleven.'

He kissed her on the cheek.

'Sorry, Ma. It's important.'

His mother looked deep into his eyes. She didn't like what she saw. His expression reminded her of the bad old days.

'You've time for a coffee,' she said firmly.

Luke made the best imitation of a smile he could. 'Coffee would help to keep me awake.'

'What's wrong?' she asked, pouring water into the kettle and flicking the switch. 'What's so important you've got to go out this time of night? It's nothing to do with Shuna is it?' Mrs Harrison had always adopted a no-interference policy in her son's personal life. Shuna was the exception to her golden rule. Luke had kept them apart — which was wise. Non-interfering she may be, but Mrs Harrison had wanted to strangle the girl on more than one occasion. She hoped the latest rumours weren't true.

Luke shook his head. 'It's not Shuna.'

'The baby's not yours then I take it, or is she up to her old tricks again?'

Her words sent an oath flying from Luke's lips that should have shocked his mother, but only brought relief. Clearly he hadn't known about the baby.

'Sorry,' he apologised hastily, mopping up the contents of his coffee mug.

'Sit down before you fall down, Luke,' his mother ordered, passing him a fresh mug. 'I've made it black to keep you awake. Now, what's all this about?'

'Did you say baby? Shuna's pregnant?'

'Got it from a neighbour whose son works for those builders you've got doing up your house.'

'Run that past me again.'

'I can't remember his name . . . ' she caught the look in her son's eyes and hurried her story along, 'Shuna's going round saying she's pregnant.'

'If there *is* a baby, there's no way it's mine.' The agitated look was back in Luke's eyes.

Mrs Harrison took a deep breath, anxious to get her explanation over as quickly as possible.

'The other girl, Tania? The one doing up the house? According to gossip, and don't ask me how the locals know — you know what this place is like — there was a scene . . . ' Mrs Harrison hesitated. 'I think Shuna told Tania she was pregnant and, well . . . ' Another colourful oath escaped Luke's lips. 'I don't know any more.'

'She's gone,' Luke swallowed some coffee. It scalded his tongue, but he didn't notice.

'They've both gone.' Mrs Harrison wasn't sure who 'she' was.

'I've got to find her. Explain.'

'Tania is an unusual name.' Mrs Harrison's eyes met the despair in her son's eyes. Her suspicions were correct, he was still in love with the girl she could only just remember. But she knew she'd always liked her and her mother. 'Tania Jordan?' Luke nodded.

His head fell forward.

'I've got to get to London,' Luke finished his coffee and stood up.

'Not now, Luke.'

'I have to go.'

'Stay the night here then go first thing in the morning when the rain's stopped. I'll make you up a bed.'

'I can't wait Mother.'

Mrs Harrison's face creased in

concern. She'd never seen her son like this before, not even when he'd discovered Shuna had tricked him into marriage.

'If you must go, at least drive down in your car.'

'The Harley's quicker. Don't worry. Nothing will happen to me.'

Mrs Harrison knew better than to argue with her son. 'You've always done things your own way, but are you sure that it's really necessary . . . ?'

Luke picked up his helmet. 'I'll phone you from London. Don't worry.'

Mrs Harrison put a hand out and grasped his fingers. 'Tell me, Luke,' the blue eyes, a twin reflection of her son's wavered, 'it is to do with Tania Jordan, isn't it? You do love her, don't you? *Really* love her? I mean, it's not some sort of stupid vendetta thing to get even with her over Harry Fitzroy, or anything like that?'

Luke didn't move a muscle and Mrs Harrison felt a quiver of alarm. Her son was so much like his father, her first husband. He'd died before Luke had been born — in a motorbike accident — something she'd never told Luke. He'd been coming to see her on a forty-eight hour pass . . . Luke looked down at his mother and something twisted in his heart. He hated to do this to her, but he hadn't thought it was possible to love another female as much as he loved her. She'd lost two husbands but, underneath it all, she was a strong woman — like Tania. Which was why he couldn't let Tania slip through his fingers over a stupid misunderstanding.

'Yes, I really love her,' he said. 'And it's time to tell her — everything.'

Mrs Harrison reached up and stroked his rain-wet hair. Luke had outgrown her height in his teenage years but he was still her son, the baby she'd held in her arms as she'd cried for his father.

'What kept you so long?'

'You know what.'

'Pah. I've never taken the slightest

notice of any gossip.'

Luke squeezed her shoulder, his eyes rueful and with an incredibly gentle smile said, 'That's my girl.'

'Just come back safely — both of you.'

She watched him stride out to his motorbike, the security system on the block of flats highlighting the brightly painted flames on the bodywork. He turned to look back at her. She gave him a little wave, making sure her hand didn't tremble. It would never do to let him see she worried about him. She'd been lying when she said she didn't. But worry about him or not, Luke was his own man.

It was still raining hard as Luke headed back to the M4. His head throbbed, but he was damned if he was going to give in to the bone-weary tiredness that was making every limb in his body ache. He'd got to get to Tania. He'd got to explain. He'd bought The Peacock House for her. He wanted to see her face the first morning they woke up together and looked out on the lawn. She said she'd love to see the sun rise. He'd personally order the best sunrise possible — if only . . .

He didn't see the lorry in front slam on its brakes as a high-performance car weaved across the slow lane to the motorway exit. He didn't hear the screech of brakes or see the lorry jack-knife until it was too late.

There was a flash of vermilion and then everything went black.

11

Tania nursed an ice-cold glass of wine and watched the ferns tremble as rabbits gambolled in and out of the greenery at the bottom of Ellie's garden. It was the first seriously warm day of summer, and her skin responded to the late afternoon sunshine. It was the only thing about her body that did feel good. She ached physically and mentally all over, except for the part of her anatomy where her heart was supposed to be. That was dead.

'Nibbles?' Ellie placed a tray of nuts and carrot sticks on the garden table, adjusted the parasol to protect her fair skin from the heat, and sat down.

The two sisters were as unlike one another as it was possible to be. Ellie, blonde, petite, and fair-skinned was a complete contrast to Tania, who was tall and dark-haired. Their characters, too, were at opposite ends of the scale. Ellie was an explosive firecracker, ready to do murder at the drop of a hat if anyone upset her or her family. Tania was a closed book. Slow to anger, she kept her feelings to herself. And that was what was worrying Ellie. The shadows were so dark under Tania's eyes she looked like she'd been punched in the face — and her body was a mass of bruises.

'You look dreadful,' she said bluntly. 'Have you been in a fight?'

'Thanks. And yes,' Tania replied, helping herself to a carrot stick. She couldn't answer Ellie's questions if she was eating properly, and she knew there were scores of them ready to tumble from Ellie's inquisitive lips. No matter how she massaged the facts, they wouldn't look good — from the fight on the kitchen floor with Shuna, to the equally vigorous activities with Luke — also on the kitchen floor!

Unusually for Ellie, she took the hint. 'Sleep well?' was all she asked.

Tania had arrived late the night before, hammering on Ellie's door at midnight. Ellie had taken one look at her sister and, without a word, heated milk, laced it liberally with brandy, forced her to drink it, then tipped her, semi-senseless into bed, giving her one of the boy's teddies to hug. Ellie had crept into the room throughout the day, eventually waking Tania for a cup of tea after she'd been asleep for eighteen hours, and removing the twin's soft toy. It was wet. Tania had been unconsciously crying in her sleep. That was what worried Ellie more than anything. Tania was tough. Tania never cried. The unwritten rule was it was Ellie who cried on Tania, not the other way round. Ellie's eyes narrowed to shards of ice. If Luke Sinclair so much as showed his face round here, she'd do something unmentionable to his manhood. Tania was the best sister in the world and, if Luke had harmed a hair of her head, she'd swing for him.

Tania had eyed the moist fur of the

toy Ellie was clutching over the rim of her cup of tea, but hadn't said a word. Ellie had closed the door with the words, 'Have a shower. It's a lovely evening and we'll have a drink in the garden.'

'Are you going to tell me about it?' she asked as the silence between them lengthened.

'Not ready yet, Ellie.'

The tears on the teddy bear had been tears of rage, Tania had lectured herself in the shower — rage with herself — nothing else. She'd scrubbed hard at her flesh, but nothing could cleanse the stains on her heart. The bruise on her thigh mocked her, reminding her what Luke had done to her body.

'I understand,' Ellie nodded. 'If it's any help, I'm on your side, no matter what. You don't have to pretty the story up for my benefit.'

Washed out as she was, Tania couldn't help smiling. Ellie drove her up the wall frequently. She was a nosey, interfering, bossy little squirt who had always got under her skin. Yet . . . Tania shook her head. She'd got enough emotion to get through without going all gooey over Ellie. And no amount of fabrication would improve her tale. It wasn't for delicate ears — like Ellie's.

'I've been a fool,' Tania confessed, a wry twist to her lips, 'the details don't matter.'

'Know the feeling.'

'Do you?' Tania turned on Ellie, the poison dart of the question widening her sister's eyes to blue circle saucers.

'Of . . . of course. We've all done . . . '

'You haven't.' Tania made a harsh, pheasant-type croaking noise. 'You left school at eighteen, married Charles, within a year. He's loaded, adores the ground you walk on, and you've been blessed with the most beautiful twin boys imaginable. How can you possibly understand . . . ?'

'Hold it. Hold it.' Ellie's blue eyes, never very good at being passive, now sparkled with their own brand of anger.

Tania bit her lip. 'Sorry.' She snatched another carrot stick, and crunched it viciously. 'Shouldn't have said that.' It wasn't fair to take it out on Ellie. In her way, she was only trying to help.

'No, you shouldn't. So, you've loused up. Big deal. Haven't we all? Do you think it's easy being married to a man like Charles? Having to look like this?' Tania's eyes flickered in disbelief over Ellie's matching shirt and shorts. Her finger and toenails were perfectly manicured and her hair shone with the latest low-light blonde. 'It's high maintenance.'

'You're breaking my heart.' Feeling as lousy as she was, Tania couldn't resist the sarcastic retaliation. She'd forgotten how self-centred her sister could be. It provided a welcome break from her own problems.

'Charles wouldn't marry me,' the slight went unnoticed by Ellie, 'so I had to get myself pregnant. Twin boys were an added bonus. Went down well with

261

his mother. She absolutely dotes on them.'

'What are you complaining about then?'

'Because to get Charles to do anything, means giving him a great big shove. I sent him away because he's driving me up the wall. Must be something to do with his job. Can you imagine anything more boring than a commodity broker?'

Tania choked on her glass of wine. If only Luke had been boring . . . No. She mustn't go down that road. 'What . . . ?' Her question was cut short.

'Oh, I love him, more than life itself, but sometimes he's such a pompous, bull-headed, self-opinionated bore. I could throttle him.'

'That's pretty comprehensive.' Talking to Ellie about Charles did help to ease her pain. She had to get on with her own life now that Luke was no longer a part of it. If Ellie wanted to sound off about Charles, then Tania was prepared to listen. It saved her the trouble of talking.

'His mother's the same. Must be in the genes. So,' she shrugged, 'I ditched him for the weekend — the boys too. I'm all yours.' She downed her drink in one long swallow and splashed more wine into both their glasses. 'I've been working hard on your behalf, Tania. Ear-bending from you I do not need.'

Ellie's raised voice sent a squawk of alarm round the garden, as the birds flew off into the trees and the rabbits made a run for it into the undergrowth. Only Ellie's lazy cocker spaniel snoozed through the sisterly scrap.

Tania took a deep breath. 'Now that you've got that off your chest, shall we start again? You know I'm no good at arguing, especially with you.'

'Agreed.' It was in Ellie's favour, she never bore a grudge. 'Besides you always lose,' Ellie grabbed a handful of nuts. 'Blow the diet. We've got chicken in the creamiest sauce you can imagine for dinner, followed by your favourite calorie-laden blackberry tart. Now, what have I said?' She stopped the peanut-filled palm halfway to her mouth. 'For heaven's sake, Tania, get a grip. You're turning into a bore. I've never known you like this.'

Tania had never known herself like this either. 'Not very hungry,' she managed to mumble. She'd never eat blackberry tart again or poached salmon!

'Come on. It'd take more than a mention of blackberry tart to do that to your face. Want me to get a mirror?'

Tania could imagine how she looked without the aid of a mirror. She really must pull herself together. Luke Sinclair was probably at this moment with Shuna on some expensive yacht laughing his head off about her, looking forward to the birth of their baby.

'I don't think I could manage blackberry tart, that's all.'

'You've got to eat something. When did you last have a decent meal?'

Tania could feel hysteria bubbling up

inside her. There'd been the langoustines she'd shared with Luke — but
decent? Definitely not. She closed her
eyes, recalling the smell of the garlic
butter, the fish shells, and their two
sex-heated bodies rolling round the
floor. Her temperature rocketed. The
hell of it was she'd do it all again given
the chance.

'I had a meal with Luke in The
Feathers.' Tania couldn't remember
how many nights ago it had been.
Three? Four? She'd spent one day at
The Peacock House working on auto-
matic pilot after Shuna had gone. Then
she'd driven 'hell for leather' back to
her studio. She couldn't remember how
long it had taken to get to Ellie's house.
Just getting through one day at a time
had been her top priority. Her stomach
had rejected food. And now half a glass
of wine was making her feel light-
headed. She nibbled a few peanuts to
satisfy Ellie, as the garden held its
breath. It was the first time Tania had
mentioned *the* name.

'Is this what it's all about?' Ellie asked softly. 'Luke?'

Tania nodded slowly. There was no point in denying it. 'I've . . . '

'If it hurts, I don't want to know,' Ellie held up a hand.

'Wasn't . . . ' Tania bit down the rest of her reply as unnatural laughter again bubbled to her lips. She could just imagine the expression on Ellie's face if she did tell all. For all her spunk, Ellie was quite conventional, with her mock-Tudor residence in commuter belt Surrey, and respectable neighbours.

'Because I may just murder him if I know the details.'

'Why? He's done nothing to you.'

Ellie's rosebud-pink lips suddenly looked as though they had developed thorns.

'He didn't give you those bruises?'

'None that you can see,' Tania said, thinking of the one at the top of her thigh.

'Is it safe for me to talk about *him*?' Ellie spoke in italics, despite her

266

apparent indifference, eyes on fire with curiosity.

'Why not? Now's as good a time as any.'

'I don't think there will ever be a good time to say what I've got to say.'

'Might as well get it out your system, then we can talk about something else. After tonight, I don't intend to ever mention his name again. OK?'

'You may have to,' Ellie said with an unhappy frown. 'Luke Sinclair isn't all he appears to be.' Tania was busy rubbing the deepest purple bruise on her arm. It was difficult to shake off the habit of not listening to Ellie. They had different priorities in their lives and, what was important to Ellie, usually wasn't important to Tania. She'd probably discovered Luke had had a fling with some minor celebrity. Celebrity gossip was high on Ellie's rating of importance. 'Are you listening, Tania?' Ellie pelted her with a handful of nuts. The cocker spaniel opened a lazy eye, ambled across the grass, ate a few, sniffed the rest, and then fell back asleep.

'Pack it in. Yes, I'm listening.' Tania stopped looking at her bruises and removed peanuts from her hair.

'He was married to Shuna S, the face of 'Millennium' cosmetics. You know that, don't you?'

'Yes.' Tania composed her face into what she hoped was an expression of interest. Shuna was another name she didn't intend ever mentioning again.

'I blame myself for not recognising him at that dinner party. But he came over so strong — well, I was flattered to be honest.'

'Sounds like his style — All charm, no substance.'

Ellie ignored the interruption. 'Those eyes, that smile!' Tania gripped the stem of her wine glass. 'Careful, they're expensive.' Ellie nodded towards Tania white knuckles. Tania loosened her grip fractionally. 'Where was I?'

'I don't need a list of Luke Sinclair's plus points, Ellie.'

'He made me want to rip my dress off, I can tell you. Charles was livid when we got home. Said I'd behaved disgracefully. I told him sucks to that! We had a row.'

'Entertaining as this is . . . ' Tania lost the battle with good manners. 'Can we change the subject?'

'Seriously, Sis, it wasn't just my imagination. I know I can knock 'em dead without trying . . . sorry.' She held up a hand. 'The hostess let slip Luke had asked to sit next to me. According to her, he'd virtually wangled himself an invitation to the party as well, through some vague business acquaintance. What do you make of that?'

Was there any female safe from Luke Sinclair? Tania thought bitterly. He appeared to have a string of them. There was the one answering his telephone in America, Shuna, now Ellie. Tania had obviously been an amusing little interlude to pass the time while he sorted things out with Shuna.

'Tania?'

'No comment,' she said dryly, holding out her glass for a refill.

'Like that, is it?'

'Worse.'

'Of course, it does all make sense. You see . . . drat.' Ellie spilt some wine as the telephone shrilled. 'Charles, darling. How are you? Good,' she made a face at Tania, who looked away with a tired smile. 'The boys behaving?' There followed a few moments domestic exchange, convincing Tania — not that she'd been worried in the first place — that everything was fine with the Charles and Ellie marriage. Ellie, as usual, had over-dramatised the situation, something Tania realised she ought to have remembered, another thing her sister was good at. 'Tania's here. Yes. Great, isn't it. What? Oh, just a drink in the garden. You know, darling, one before supper.' She crossed her eyes in Tania's direction, a habit of hers since childhood when she tried to tell a lie. 'No, of course not. We're going inside soon. Got some chicken. What was that? The news. No. I told you, we're in the garden. Why?' There was a long silence. Ellie looked across at Tania's turned head and gripped the receiver hard. 'Are you sure?' She lowered her voice and turned her own head away from Tania's. 'I mean, there's no mistake?' She listened for a second. 'Last night? Where?' Another pause. 'Oh my God. What do you think I should do? Charles,' Ellie hissed, 'what? Your mother?' Ellie's voice was back at full decibel level. 'Oh right. Can't keep her waiting. No. Don't bother. Sort it out myself. Thanks for calling. Love you. Kiss the boys for me. Yes. Next week.' She switched off and took a long swallow of wine.

Tania turned her attention from the rabbits back to face her sister. What on earth had happened to Ellie? Her face was stripped of colour and her eyes looked waterlogged, as if she was holding back tears. It must be a blip of the evening sun, Tania thought. Nothing was normal tonight.

'Charles is OK?' Guilt-ridden, Tania asked the question. Perhaps she should have taken Ellie's whinging a bit more seriously. 'It's not the boys, is it?'

Ellie hesitated. 'No, everything's fine. Absolutely. They send their love by the way.'

The expression on Ellie's face didn't change, not even at the mention of her sons.

'What then?' Tania demanded. Ellie was blinking at the wine bottle. It was empty. 'Ellie?' Her sister hadn't crossed her eyes — she wasn't lying — but Tania knew she was keeping something back from her. 'What is it?' She felt a twinge of fear.

Ellie took a deep breath. 'There's something I've got to tell you, Tania.'

'Well?'

'I don't know how to start and you're not going to like it.'

'How about the beginning? And you needn't leave anything out, I can take it.'

Ellie dug a carrot baton in the

peanuts and stirred them like a cup of tea. Peanuts flew everywhere. Neither of the girls took any notice as several birds swooped on to the lawn and flapped away with their unexpected spoils.

'Remember how Charles was looking into Luke Sinclair's background?'

'Yes. He couldn't find anything out, you told me.'

'I had a go at it after Charles had given up. Remember? I tried to tell you on the telephone? Before you cut me off? What happened by the way?'

'It doesn't matter. Go on.'

'What can you tell me about Harry?'

Pain sliced through Tania's breast-bone at the mention of her first love. In all this, she'd forgotten Harry. Forgotten how he too had broken her heart. Men were the pits, Tania decided. She was never, ever, getting involved with one again. 'Singleton' status had a lot going for it.

'Harry Fitzroy?' She repeated the name numbly. 'His parents owned The

Peacock House. What's he got to do with Luke? Apart from the fact that it was Luke that bought the house?'

'I don't remember much about him. I was packed off to Cornwall, to some old aunt after . . . everything.'

Tania gave a sad smile. 'Poor Ellie. I suppose no one ever really bothered to explain things to you.'

'When I came back, you'd gone to London. Whenever I tried to ask, everyone clamped up. In the end I gave up asking.'

'There were rumours, something about one of the peacocks straying into the path of his car.'

'Were you engaged — to Harry?'

'Unofficially. Nothing would ever have come of it, I can see that now. Why?'

'I looked up past editions of the *Gazette*.'

'What for?'

'I wanted to read about The Peacock House. You know, just to find out something — anything! I was annoyed with Charles for giving up on Luke. I remembered roughly when Harry died, so I started there. It was a long shot, but it paid off.'

Tania shivered. The afternoon breeze didn't seem so warm. She grabbed her shawl and wrapped it round her shoulders.

'Are you up to this?'

'Go on.'

'Luke Sinclair's a local.' Tania blinked. Her mouth had gone dry and Ellie had gone out of focus. 'He was born in Evesham. He lived in Little Chipping . . . when we were there!'

There was the familiar blinding flash in Tania's memory. She *had* known Luke Sinclair in the past. She had recognised him that first day on that footbridge in the village. It wasn't because he was married to a super-model. It was because he'd . . . what? After Harry's death, her defence mechanism had shut out a lot of the past. What had Luke Sinclair been in her past?

'I don't remember . . . ' her forehead throbbed.

'The night Harry died, it was rumoured that someone was having a race with him on a motorbike.'

'A Harley-Davidson.' Tania's words were a groan.

'How did you know?'

'I didn't.'

'Nothing was ever proved. There were tyre marks near the scene, but they were never identified.'

'Luke drove off and left Harry?'

'They don't know that it was Luke. They don't even know there was a race. It was just a ghastly accident, but I thought you ought to know.' Ellie looked unhappy as if she wished she hadn't started her story.

'I don't remember anyone called Luke Sinclair.' Tania struggled with the shreds of her memory.

'His stepfather was Mr Harrison, the gardener at The Peacock House. In those days, he called himself Luke Harrison. Remember now?'

With a blinding flash Tania did remember. It had been Luke with her that day tying up the canes in the fruit cage. Luke, who'd fed her the luscious fruit and wiped the juice from her face with his not-very-clean hankie. How could she ever have forgotten — the smile, the eyes, and the scar? He'd even told her how he'd got it — falling out of an apple tree he'd been forbidden to climb. He'd cut his face and had to have five stitches, he'd told her proudly.

'My God, Tania. You're not going to be sick are you?'

'I don't think so,' she gasped. 'It's just the shock.'

Ellie fiddled with the telephone still lying on the table between them. 'That's not all.' She looked even unhappier.

Tania shook her head. 'I don't want to hear any more. I'm resigning this commission. I couldn't work with Luke Sinclair, not now. Not even if he paid me treble fees.'

'Don't say that, Tania.'

'Why not? It's the truth.'

'You may regret it later.'

'I regret everything about Luke Sinclair, or Harrison, or whatever the swine wants to call himself. Next time you meet someone at a dinner party, Ellie, keep me out of it.'

Ellie's head fell forward, her blonde hair falling like a curtain about her face. She searched in her shorts for a tissue and blew her nose defiantly.

'For heaven's sake, Ellie. It's me. Tania. You can turn off the taps. I'm immune.'

'That was Charles on the telephone,' she said through tear washed eyes, her voice so low Tania could hardly catch her words.

'I know that. Ellie? What's wrong?' Tania coaxed, a frown distorting her eyebrows. 'Look, I'm sorry. I shouldn't have snapped. I'm having a bad day. You've been an absolute brick and I don't know where I'd have been without you. You know that. I always say what I mean.' She touched Ellie's hand. It was freezing cold. 'Ellie?' Her sister hiccuped down more tears. 'Stop it.' She shook Ellie's fingers, wondering if she ought to slap her sister's face. Whatever had Charles said to her to get her into this state?

'It was on the news. Charles heard it.'

'Would you like some water?'

'There's been an accident on the M4.'

Tania was half out her seat. 'The M4?' she repeated stupidly. 'Accident?'

'In the rain, on the London-bound carriageway. Something to do with a lorry and a motorbike — a Harley-Davidson.'

'No.' Tania toppled back into her seat.

'It's Luke.'

'What's happened to him?'

Ellie's cocker spaniel began to bark.

'Luke skidded out-of-control and went under a lorry.'

12

The car swept into the drive of The Peacock House as the shadows from the rhododendron bushes lengthened across the lawn. Several lights twinkled from the open windows and some builders' vans were still parked on the gravel outside. Luke's legs hadn't liked the journey and his ribs felt as if they were about to walk out on him, but he didn't care. It had been a month now, the longest month of his life, since he'd seen or spoken to Tania. Even his long years away in the States had seemed like two weeks in comparison to the last month. Through flashes of pain, he remembered her face on the bridge at Little Chipping, having a bad hair day, with her skirt all stained and her leather shoes ruined. The nurses had thought his cries had been of pain. They had, but his pain had been far worse than physical, it had been mental. Did she know he'd had an accident? Had anyone told her? No one in the hospital would listen when he tried to explain, they just kept dosing him with painkillers.

The physiotherapist had almost had a stand-up argument with him when he'd insisted on discharging himself, but he knew if he'd stayed one more day at St Mary's, he'd have gone mad.

When they'd finished pumping him with injections and lacing his drinks with painkillers at the hospital, the Consultant had stipulated complete rest — no telephone calls and no visitors, apart from his next of kin. As his scarred, stitched and battered body slowly recovered, his mind went into overdrive.

'You've been in a very nasty crash,' the Senior sister had eyed him with professional steel as she took his temperature, at the same time wishing she were two stone lighter and fifteen years younger.

'There's someone I need to call — desperately,' Luke had spoken round the thermometer, almost biting the end off in his anguish.

'Absolutely not.' She felt for his pulse. It was racing. Whoever he wanted to call, she thought, was a lucky woman. And the nurse had no doubt it was a woman. She'd heard he was married to a supermodel, but his mother was listed as his next of kin. She'd replaced his chart at the end of his bed. To her relief, he was breathing deeply again from the effects of the sleeping draught. The parts of his face that weren't bruised were as white as the bed sheets. He was lucky to be alive, she thought, as she looked down at him. He wasn't handsome, but there was something about his face even the bruises couldn't hide — strong but sensitive too. He reminded her of her son when his girlfriend had thrown him over and he'd come to her for reassurance. She closed the door with a gentle sigh and hoped that whoever it was he was so deeply in love with, didn't break his heart.

There was a sharp stab of pain in Luke's chest as the car came slowly to a halt. If he closed his eyes, he could see Tania — feel the softness of her flesh, the touch of her hair, the smell of her body. It was too much for him in his weakened state. What if she wasn't here? What if his mother's contact had got it all wrong?

Beside him on the back seat, Mrs Harrison put a hand out to her son's arm as he grappled with the door handle.

'I don't need help.'

'I wasn't going to offer and may I remind you who you're talking to?' his mother asked mildly.

'Sorry.' He gave a shamefaced smile. 'I'll make it up to you, I promise.'

'Quite frankly, I'll be glad to see the back of you.' The expression in her eyes belied her words, 'Those poor nurses. How they put up with you, I don't know.'

'Sorry,' Luke ground out again. He loved his mother dearly, but right now he wasn't in the mood for maternal lectures.

'I've made a bed up for you in The Lodge. Or are you sure I can't persuade you to come back with me? All this can wait. You need rest. The Consultant wasn't happy about . . .'

Luke shook his head. Rest was absolutely the last thing he wanted. He'd had enough sleep to last him for years. And much as he loved his mother . . . 'We haven't lived together since I was eighteen. You know we'd drive each other up the wall in five minutes.'

Mrs Harrison smiled reluctantly. They were too alike, that was their problem. He leant across the back seat and kissed her. 'Thanks — for everything. I'll be in touch.'

'I can take a hint,' his mother touched his face and pretended not to notice his wince of pain. 'You know where I am if you need me.'

Luke struggled out of the car and,

nudging the door closed with his crutch, watched it circle the rose bed and the tail-lights flicker as the driver sped his mother back to her flat. As soon as Luke could, he would arrange a bouquet of fresh deep-pink carnations for her. They'd always been her, and his stepfather's, favourite flowers.

He turned and faced the house, scarcely able to breathe from the tension in his chest. The chest bandages felt several sizes too small. It had been a warm day and the heat hadn't really left the evening air. His bandages itched from the warmth of his body and his shirt stuck to his back. The journey had tired his body, but his mind was like a hamster on a wheel, going round and round relentlessly and getting nowhere. The stone, deep gold in the evening sunlight, was warm against the palm of his hand as he rested against the outer wall for a few moments to catch his breath. While he'd been in hospital, the garden had run riot. The grass was a mass of dandelions and daisies.

Cabbage roses swayed against the sunlight and, out of the corner of his eyes, he caught an orange glimpse of tiger lily. He'd planted it that first afternoon with Tania. He remembered how she'd told him it would never take and he'd mentally promised that when it did, he would pick the biggest bud he could find and present it to her, just to prove her wrong. His lips twisted in a smile. He hadn't had much to amuse him recently and it felt strange.

He raised his head and with a final pat of the wall, manipulated his crutches along the flowerbed until he reached the oak front door. He gave it a gentle nudge. It swung open at his touch. Luke hadn't felt like this since he was about twelve-years-old and been called to the head teacher's study to explain why he'd been found roller-skating in the park instead of sitting a French exam. He rubbed his sweating palms down the front of his shirt, then gripped the handles of his crutches again and eased slowly through the open door. Unused to such vigorous exercise, his legs let him know they were unhappy. Luke ignored them. He wasn't about to let trembling limbs stop him finding Tania.

Biting his lip, he hobbled into the main hallway and, looking round him, choked down a gasp of surprise. The floor was a mass of wood shavings, wiring, drills, trestle tables and pots of varnish. The tattered wall coverings had been stripped down to the original panelling and the barley sugar twists on the banisters of the oak staircase sanded down to basic wood, ready for the first coat of varnish. He inhaled the smell of the work with a throb of excitement. This was how it was meant to be. Things were still a mess, but from the raw material, Luke could see his plans were going to work. He felt an electric shock pulse through his body. All this had been done — for him. He shook the absurd feeling of wetness from his eyelashes. It had to be the medication that was making him over-react. On shaky legs he moved forward, careful not to disturb anything. A ray of evening sunlight cut a swathe across the hall and he followed its path towards the drawing room. He could hear faint movements. Someone was there. Shadows moved in the sunlight. Tania. The rush of blood to his head was deafening.

★   ★   ★

'She's at the house,' his mother had told him, once they'd allowed him to get up and he'd been staring morosely out the window, planning his escape.

Luke had jerked his head up. 'What?' The one word had been no more than an energised whisper.

'My contacts there told me she's working hard. You remember my friend with the son? Hope you intend paying overtime. That penalty clause is a killer.'

'Tania's at The Peacock House?'

'She's got the workmen eating out of her hand, even that crusty old foreman.

There's nothing they won't do for her. They're all sorry about what happened. Want to do their best for you by way of compensation.'

Until now, Luke hadn't dared believe it was true. No one had been allowed to visit him apart from his mother. He'd heard from one of the nurses that Tania had telephoned, but they hadn't put her through. Apparently her voice had sounded so hoarse, the receptionist thought she was a man, a reporter or someone from the Press, disguising his voice and pretending to be his girl-friend. Luke had been forced to make a sizeable donation to the hospital charity by way of apology to the poor girl. Not his finest hour, he thought grimly, but he'd been driven by desperation.

'And I've some even better news,' his mother had told him. 'They've agreed you can leave — with me. There was a sigh of relief all round when I suggested it. You haven't been the easiest of patients.'

Luke had fought with the blanket

covering his knees. 'Get me out of this thing. Crutches are over there. No, I'll get them.' Luke would have crawled across the floor if his mother hadn't pressed the call bell button for assistance from the nursing staff.

The administrator was not given to shock. In her forty years of hospital administration she'd seen it all, but the size of the cheque Luke Sinclair had written out for their benefit fund had raised even her eyebrows.

And now suddenly Tania was there, flesh and blood, framed in the doorway, wearing a man's shirt several sizes too big for her, her hair tied up in a dirty old handkerchief and a pot of paint in her hand. Luke's breath caught in his chest. There were sleep-starved circles of purple under her eyes, but she was more beautiful than he'd remembered. The colour drained from her face.

'Luke.' She let the paint fall from her fingers. It spattered butter yellow spots down her jeans.

He wanted to drop his crutches and

run across the hall and scoop her up in his arms. But he couldn't. He tried, but his body finally let him down. It had had enough bullying. His feet wouldn't respond to the message his brain was sending out. He threw down his sticks, moved two paces forward then, with a cry of frustration and pain, toppled to the floor on top of his crutches.

'Luke!' As he slipped on the pool of paint, he heard Tania scream his name.

Covered in yellow paint and feeling faintly ridiculous, he tried to tell her that he was all right. He wanted to laugh, he was just so happy at having found her again but, as she threw her own body on to the floor beside his and cradled his paint-bespattered head in her arms, he never wanted to move or speak again. She smelt wonderful — a mixture of paint, grubby shirt, dust and . . . he sniffed gently, tears? His face was wet from hers as she touched her cheek against his. He trembled in her arms. Did he dare hope the tears were for him? His body stirred in a way he'd only ever dreamed about before.

'Darling, are you all right?'

Something incredibly soft and feminine was being pushed against his face. Luke rested his cheek against the trembling cushion of her breasts.

He didn't want to open his eyes, so he stayed where he was. Had Tania really called him darling? Had he died and gone to heaven? If he didn't move, perhaps she'd . . .

'Luke.' He could feel her fingers tracing the scars on his face. 'Luke. Say something.'

Her scent was so arousing and far more erotic than anything 'Millennium Cosmetics' could produce. He rolled his head sideways and gently kissed a button on the front of her shirt. It was loose and came undone from the buttonhole as he disturbed it with his lips. She wasn't wearing a bra. He almost blacked out as his lips now came into contact with one of her breasts. It felt soft and creamy. Unable to stop himself, he nibbled the tender flesh and

Tania bent her head forward on a gasp of pain as his teeth nicked her nipple. Her hair tickled his face. It was too much for his manhood.

'Help me,' he rasped, struggling now, unable to wait much longer. If they didn't do something soon he'd die of embarrassment. He gritted his teeth. She didn't seem to be getting his drift.

'Your poor face,' she said still stroking his designer stubble. He hadn't bothered to shave well in hospital. It had all been too much of an effort and it helped disguise the bruises. The sensation of her fingertips against his five o'clock shadow was sending his senses into orbit. 'It looks like an unfinished tapestry.' She traced a line of stitch-marks with a delicate forefinger.

'Damn my face,' Luke's words burnt his own vocal chords and made Tania blush, 'if you don't help me . . . '

'What do you want me to do? Do you want to get up?'

'No I don't. I want to make love to

you — here, now. And I can't wait much longer.'

Her hands were now undoing his shirt and he heard her indrawn breath as she saw his bandages.

'Luke, no. I can't.'

'Yes,' he insisted. 'Damned legs, here, you do it.' No longer lazy against her chest, he struggled with the belt of his jeans. He'd lost weight in hospital. They were too big for him and with Tania's help easily slid down his legs.

In a miracle of need, he managed to shed his clothes.

'We can't,' she protested, 'you should be in bed.'

'Isn't time.'

'Then not on the floor — again!'

'I'm not moving,' he growled in her ear, then savagely yanked off her headscarf, the only article of clothing she appeared to be wearing.

'There's some old carpet I've been using . . .'

'No time,' Luke insisted.

In a daze, Tania felt him begin

rhythmic movements inside her body. She'd no idea how she'd positioned herself under him, she just knew she didn't want him to stop. She made a funny little sound like a kitten squealing. It turned harsher and more demanding as Luke's climax thrust him harder and harder into her femininity. She clung to him as they shuddered together in the final throes of their lifeline to each other, then with one final huge sob of escaping breath, Luke fell back on to the floor bringing Tania over on top of him. The parts of his body not covered in bandages stuck to hers. They clung to each other, both exhausted, both gasping for air until Luke opened his eyes and grinned into Tania's.

'Do you always greet friends like this when you haven't seen them for a while?' She stiffened in his arms as reality entered the situation and tried to escape from the padlock of his arms. 'Don't go all prickly.'

'I'm not.'

'Yes, you are.' He kissed the tip of her nose. 'It's gone red. Just like a ripe cherry.' His blue eyes moved down her flesh. 'Other parts of your body are . . . excited too.'

'Luke.' She began wriggling harder, flooded with embarrassment.

'Stop it. You're hurting me,' he protested.

'I don't care.'

'I'm not letting you go, so it's no good protesting. We've got a lot of catching up to do. You don't know how I've dreamt of this moment, stuck in that hospital bed with hatchet-faced nurses whose greatest pleasure in life was lacing my drinks with ghastly stuff to knock me out, and then when that didn't work, sticking needles into the most tender part of your anatomy. You've no idea . . . '

'Luke,' the tone of Tania's voice grew more urgent.

'You don't seem awfully interested in . . . '

'I'm not.'

Luke's face suddenly looked like a finished tapestry. All the loose ends of his injuries disappeared, as he gave his first real smile for weeks.

'Nice to know you care.'

'For goodness sake.' He wanted to drown in the depths of her amethyst eyes. 'Will you stop?'

'No.'

'Luke.'

'You are a fidget. What on earth's the matter?' He punctuated his question with kisses down the side of her face. His hands lingered over her ribs. 'You've lost weight.' His voice was softer now. 'How about a salmon and blackberry tart supper in The Feathers? Or, perhaps you'd prefer something else for dessert?'

'The builders.'

'I don't think they're on the menu, but if you insist . . . '

Tania was breathing heavily and shaking his shoulders. 'Stop it. Listen.'

'Ouch that hurts. You're going to pay for that when I'm better.'

'The builders.'

'What is it between you and the builders? And there's no need to shout. I haven't gone deaf. My ears are in working order, so is my . . . '

'They're out the back.'

'So? They can wait. Grateful as I am for what they've done, I'm not about to go out there like this and thank them.'

'For heaven's sake, put your clothes on.'

'Why? I like the feel of your warm body against mine. In fact, I might just stay here all night.'

'Don't you understand? The builders . . . '

'They're not about to burst in on us, are they?'

'Yes.' If Tania had been in the mood she would have laughed at the expression of dismay on Luke's face. 'They've only gone for a quick tea break. They'll be back any minute. They don't go home at night any more. They mustn't find us here like this.'

'Shh . . . I mean why didn't you tell me before?'

'You didn't give me a chance. Besides, you had other things on your mind.'

Luke grinned. 'If you're interested in an action replay . . . '

'No, I'm not. Hurry up. The security guard's due as well any minute.'

'Why didn't you pay the wretched man off? There are far too many people around as it is.'

'Because he's been helping too.'

'He what?'

'I haven't time to tell you all that's been happening. Just get dressed.'

Luke tried to get to his jeans, but they were too far away. 'It's no good.' He gave up. 'I can't reach them.'

The sound of laughing male voices grew louder and closer. Tania froze. Luke lay back on the uncarpeted floor, totally naked except for his bandages and socks, and burst into laughter.

'It's not funny.' Tania looked ready to burst into tears. 'Do something.'

'Like what?'

'Get up. Anything. Don't just lie there — like that.'

'Can't. My legs won't work properly.'

With a whimper of panic, Tania threw his shirt and jeans over him and, picking up her discarded clothes, fled into the drawing room.

13

'Do you realise this is a first?' Luke leaned over and kissed Tania's naked shoulder.

She felt a flood of feminine desire as the blue eyes mocked hers.

'First?'

'I know you usually prefer the floor, but I thought it was time for a little more civilised behaviour . . . ' His teasing was cut off mid-sentence. 'Tania. For pity's sake, mind my bandages. Agh! You witch.' Despite his injuries, he held her down by the wrists, his legs straddling hers. Breathing heavily, he punctuated his words with delicate kisses on her damp face. 'You really will have to learn some socially acceptable behaviour or is this normal for interior designers? I've led a sheltered life.'

She struggled ineffectually against

the bonds of his fingers round her wrists. 'I mean, what those builders must have thought.'

Tania went scarlet at the memory of the undignified incident, but Luke wasn't about to let her off the hook lightly. 'And talk about rats deserting a sinking ship, I've never seen you move so fast in years. Do you know your backside wobbles when you run by the way?'

'Don't remind me and shut up you beast. You've got more than your fair share of funny-shaped bits.'

'I will always remind you, right up until the day you're a very respectable matron with hordes of grandchildren who think they invented sex.'

Tania felt a funny little tremble in her stomach. She didn't, wouldn't, and couldn't, think about that day — it would never come.

'I couldn't stay there on the floor,' she tried a jokey little voice, and prayed it worked — anything to distract him from talking about the future. 'In your absence the men have been thinking of me as the boss. It's not been easy ordering round men who are used to male bosses.'

'There you go again,' Luke gave a mock sigh, 'lowering the tone.'

'I couldn't have them see me rolling round the floor . . . ' She bit her lip, flooded with embarrassment as wave after wave of shame washed over her. She'd just been so unutterably stunned then relieved to see Luke standing there and then, when he'd fallen over, death-mask white and crying her name, she'd thought, really thought, he was dying. What had happened afterwards had been instinctive. After all the weeks of uncertainty, they'd come together at a mutual point on some sort of scale of need, a top ten really. 'I had to make a bolt for it,' she said, half to herself, half to Luke.

'See your point.' Luke gave a low laugh that had Tania squirming under the pressure of his body. It was difficult to concentrate on what he was saying with his flesh so close to hers. 'Glad you weren't on the Titanic is all I can say.'

'Stop being so noble . . . '

'Doesn't matter what they thought of me then? Struggling to get my shirt on, with my trousers all undone.' Luke grinned wickedly. 'Not sure they were entirely convinced by my story, but they swallowed it in a sort of laddish understanding.'

'They knew?'

'Of course they knew.'

'What did you tell them?' Tania's eyes were enormous with curiosity.

'Just that you and I fancied a bit . . . No. Not my bandages again. Only joking. Honest. Mind my bruises. You sadist. That hurt.'

'It was meant to.'

'I'll make you pay for that when I'm up and running properly.'

'What did you tell them?' Tania demanded. How would she ever face them again knowing they knew, she knew, they knew . . . ?

'What?' Luke stopped nibbling her

ear lobe to reply. 'Said my bandages hurt so I undid my shirt and because the trousers were a bit loose, they fell down too.'

Tania bubbled up with laughter, her chest heaving against the muscle wall of Luke's bandages. 'Was that the best you could do?'

'All right,' Luke said testily. 'I was thinking on my feet. Oh shut up,' he howled as he realised what he'd said. 'There's no need to remind me I was flat on my back.'

His face was so close to Tania's now that she could see his small white scar in fine detail. The other scars were beginning to fade. She stopped laughing, memory swallowing her amusement.

Luke was on to her vibes immediately. 'Tania?'

'That scar,' she struggled free of his fingers and touched it gently. Luke flinched. 'I got it as a boy.'

'Falling out of a tree.'

Luke sank back on to his knees, his

eyes raking Tania's face. He rolled slowly over to his side of the bed. He was breathing raggedly, as if he was in pain. Tania eased her damp body away from the sheets. 'You know?'

'Why didn't you tell me who you were?'

In the half-light, Luke's face seemed to be carved of stone. He reminded Tania of some garden statues she'd been forced to tolerate when a customer had demanded they be placed at strategic points in his garden, under outdoor spotlighting. Tania hadn't liked them at all. And she didn't like the expression on Luke's face now.

'How much do you remember?'

'Not a lot. I didn't remember at all until Ellie told me.'

'I made quite an impression on you then?' There was none of the teasing lover about Luke now. His body language was all pain.

Tania shook her head. 'It wasn't like that.' She wasn't looking at Luke now. Her eyes were drawn to the three-quarters moon responsible for the eerie shapes in The Lodge bedroom. 'When Harry died, I sort of blanked out. There are large gaps, bits of my past I don't, still can't, recall. I expect there's some medical term for it. The body closing down to protect itself in fail-safe mode.'

'How does Ellie remember? She's younger than you.'

Tania didn't want to tell Luke, but she knew she had to. 'She ran a search on you.'

'She what?'

'When . . . ' Heavens, this was difficult, thought Tania, one wrong word could cause a minefield explosion. 'That dinner party, where you met her, you made sure you sat next to her. She was flattered but then smelt a rat.'

Luke didn't look quite as angry as she'd expected. Tania sensed his muscles relax. What had he been scared of her finding out? The accident? The motorbike marks on the grass verge? Their relationship was too fragile to go down that route yet — but until they did, Tania knew they would have no future together. That's why it was useless believing in jokes about grand-children.

'Oh that. Came over a bit heavy, did I? I was never very good at chatting up women, especially blondes. Not my scene. My weakness is a chestnut-haired beauty,' he tweaked an intimate part of her anatomy and Tania slapped his hand away, 'with a wobbly bottom.'

'My sister may be a blonde airhead, Luke, but she's nobody's fool. She knew the thing was rigged. The hostess told her as much. At first, she tried to get Charles to find out about you, but he drew a blank apart from a few bits about your business empire. But once Ellie's got a bee in her bonnet, there's no stopping her.' Tania flicked a glance in his direction.

'Go on.' The trapped animal wariness was back in his eyes.

'So she did her own thing and ran a search on The Peacock House.' Tania began to run her words together, something she always did when she was nervous. 'Old copies of the *Gazette* are available. You know, the local paper.'

'And?'

'It was all there.'

'What was?'

'Harry's accident. The inquest. Everything. That's when I remembered.'

'Exactly what did you remember?'

'That it was you.'

'I wasn't at the inquest,' he said in a voice devoid of emotion.

'In the fruit cage.'

She heard Luke breathe out, a long low breath as if his lungs weren't working properly. 'I wiped the juice from your chin,' Luke said softly. 'You'd stuffed an enormous gooseberry into your mouth. It was so big it made your eyes bulge. Pips and juice went everywhere.'

'Mr Harrison was your stepfather, wasn't he?'

Luke gave another long drawn-out

sigh. 'Yes. I used to help him out in the holidays. He was the gardener.'

'And you called yourself Luke Harrison in those days.'

'He never officially adopted me and, when he died, I went back to using my own father's name again.'

'Why?'

'It . . . was better that way.'

Tania knew he was covering up. She now shivered with cold. She'd given him every opportunity to confess about his part in the accident, but he hadn't said anything, not one word. She'd led him to believe she didn't remember, didn't know what had happened — and he'd chosen not to tell her.

'Why?' she asked again.

'I went to America. My passport had to be in my real name. Then the business took off and Luke Harrison was like yesterday. There's no big deal to it. But I never forgot my roots. I always knew one day I'd come back and look for the girl who gorged on gooseberries and loved peacocks, and watching the sun rise.'

Tania's throat ached from the lump of disappointment lodged firmly in her vocal chords. She desperately wanted to believe in Luke, that he was innocent of any involvement in Harry's accident, but he wasn't giving her the chance. What else could he be covering up? Why wasn't he telling her? He didn't trust her to believe him. That was the only explanation.

'America's a wonderful place, but I always knew I'd come back. The hi-tech world won't miss me,' he tweaked a strand of her hair, playing it against her cheek. 'Roots and all that. Wanted to feel earth under my fingernails again — that sort of thing. So, there it is. My story. Sorry I didn't tell you. Somehow the time was never right.'

Tania rested her head on her drawn-up knees, cradling them with her arms. Her disappointment began at her feet, worked its way up her body until she almost cried out with the pain.

'Tania?' He shook her arm gently. 'What is it?'

'I want to believe you,' she confessed. 'But there's so much you're not telling me.'

'It hardly matters now, does it?' Luke butted in. 'It was all so long ago. 'We've got to look to the future. Not the past.'

'Some bits of the past won't die.'

'Do you want me to tell you the truth?' he asked in a voice she didn't recognise. 'Is that it?'

Tania nodded against her knees, now not sure if she was ready for it. The next few minutes would change her life forever.

'Yes.'

'I think I half fell in love with you that day with your knees all scratched from the garden and your hair all over the place, much like it is now. But you were only what, fourteen?'

'Thirteen.'

Luke nodded. 'I stayed out your way while you grew up. Did all the things a man's supposed to do, things you don't

312

want to hear about, but I got myself a bit of a local reputation. Then, before I knew it, it was too late and you were all over Harry Fitzroy. I hated him for that. You see, I knew what he was really like. I was no saint, but he was . . . '

'Don't . . . don't go on.' This wasn't what she wanted to hear, but Luke didn't take any notice.

Absently he traced a finger down her spine. Tania arched her back. If he didn't stop doing that, she'd jump him. 'When I saw how it was, had been, between you and him I wasn't going to stick around to be second best . . . '

'Is that the only reason you went to America?' She fought to keep her mind on track. He had to tell her now.

'Why else?'

Tania closed her eyes. She didn't want Luke using them as a mirror to her soul. She'd never been any good at hiding her feelings and he'd know instantly that she didn't believe him. The rumours had to be true. Why else wasn't he telling her about them?

'The accident? That was why you left, wasn't it?'

'I'd already made my plans before the accident. I just hurried them along. You went away and there didn't seem much point in staying. Everything changed.'

'There were rumours ... about Harry.'

Outside she heard night noises — leaves rustling, a vixen sounding like she was being murdered, then a squeak, then silence. Inside, all she could hear was Luke's laboured breathing. A sharp stab in her own chest and black spots before her eyes, reminded her she'd forgotten to breathe.

'What sort of rumours?' Luke asked eventually.

'He wasn't alone when the car skidded.'

'He was with that girl from the village.' Luke turned his bruised, shadowed eyes away from Tania. 'I suppose we all died a little bit that day. Want to change the subject?' he

314

asked after a pause.

No, Tania wanted to scream at him. I want you to tell me it isn't true. I want you to tell me you weren't racing Harry — that the accident wasn't your fault. It wasn't your bike's tracks they found in the grass. But she couldn't. Despising herself for her weakness, she said nothing.

'I know it's difficult to understand,' Luke took her silence as assent, 'but I always loved The Peacock House. It held such happy memories. You feel like that too, don't you?' He turned back to Tania. 'You're only supposed to remember the good bits about the past and it's always been like that with me. That's why I angled for an invitation to that ghastly dinner party where I met Ellie. I knew Charles would be there, and I knew he was married to your sister. I never gave up hope that one day things would be different between us. You and I would be back here together.'

'No, Luke. We don't have a future

315

here. There are too many shadows to haunt us.'

'Only if we let them.'

'Anyway, wasn't it you who kept banging on about no commitment?' Tania was grasping at lifelines. She couldn't stay here, not now, not knowing for sure. Luke was hard-headed, single-minded, that was why he was so successful. He wouldn't let a skeleton from his past stop him getting what he really wanted. She had to get away before he broke down her resistance. Why had he come back into her life? Why hadn't he left her alone where she was? Set in her ways, single, not exactly happy, but not unhappy. She had her work and her studio. She didn't need anything else. Life had passed her by Ellie would say. So what? thought Tania. From her experience, it was no great shakes. In a few more years, she'd probably get a cat and settle down to respectable spinster-hood. Making love on the floor, any floor, would not feature in her agenda.

'You'd broken my heart once. I wasn't about to let you do it again. Something to do with macho pride I suppose.'

'Broken your heart?' Tania repeated in disbelief.

'Everyone knew you and Harry were an item.'

'I hardly knew you. I didn't even remember you.'

'There's no need to rub it in.'

'And you seem to have forgotten Shuna. Why did you marry her?'

'Is that what's worrying you?' Luke's brow darkened. 'We met at one of those celebrity things they're so fond of in the States. I suppose that I was flattered by her attention. I hadn't had a woman in a while. Don't look at me like that. I'm only a normal red-blooded male and Shuna came on pretty strong. She tricked me into marrying her, said she was expecting a baby and, since I thought I'd never have you, I thought at least I'd have a family. I paid heavily for that mistake.

She wasn't pregnant then. She isn't now. A baby would ruin her figure. Remember how she was about the Harley? That day with the peacocks? Valuable piece of machinery. That's Shuna. She bled me dry. No way am I letting her back into my life.'

'She told me you were getting back together and the baby was yours.'

'No way. You don't catch a second dose of Shuna.'

Luke's fingertips had roamed to the soft skin on the edge of her breasts. Tania felt her teeth puncture the flesh on her lower lip. She drew the sheet closer to her.

'What's the matter?' Luke asked, 'Don't you believe me?'

'Shuna said your accident was my fault . . . '

Tania shuddered as she recalled the way Shuna had snatched the telephone from the receptionist at the nursing home when Tania had tried to be put through to Luke. Shuna had been hanging round the desk trying to get in to see Luke and caught the telephone call.

'What?'

Tania felt a tiny warm glow deep inside. She was finally beginning to believe in Luke. If he'd just take her that one step further, trust her the whole way, tell her . . . everything.

Tania felt the mattress shift under Luke's weight as he moved towards her. 'Why are we wasting time talking about Shuna? She's not part of my life anymore. She never was. I told you she just followed me here because that boyfriend of hers had found himself someone else. Shuna's not the sort of female you do that to and live. I wouldn't like to be in his shoes.'

'Where is she now?'

Luke shrugged. 'No idea.' He eased himself into a more comfortable position. 'You haven't explained what you're doing here.' He played with a curl of her hair, tickling her ear. 'Last thing I recall, was that you were going to stay out of my life forever.'

Tania swayed, suddenly very tired. She'd been working eighteen-hour days for weeks now. She'd lost count of how many. Her life was a blur of work, coffee, snatched snacks, minimal sleep, and endless problems.

'I was staying with Ellie when the news came through about your accident.'

'I was coming to find you,' Luke admitted.

'Then it was my fault.'

'Stop blaming yourself. I was the fool still suffering from jet lag and not paying attention. I was the one who went under the lorry. The accident was my fault, no one else's. Period. I'm just grateful that I was the only idiot injured.'

Tania was so tired now she could hardly think straight. What had happened? Why had she come back?

'I still had your house keys. I found them in my bag when I went back to my studio. I didn't know what to do. I telephoned the hospital, but they wouldn't let me speak to you. Then, when Shuna told me she'd put the police on to me unless I stopped stalking you . . . '

'She what?' Luke yelped making Tania jump.

'I was so angry with her, with you, that stupid bike, that I came back here. I was going to post your keys through the lodge door, but the security guard was here. So, I tried to give them to him instead. He wouldn't accept them. Then the builders began arriving. I must have driven through the night. I don't remember clearly.'

'You are never to do that again,' Luke said in a voice that melted her insides.

'When they saw me, they sort of thought I was in charge. Nobody knew what was going on, the place was in uproar. The foreman had stood guarantor for everything so, as I had your authority to redecorate, I was on a commission and the hospital assured me you weren't about to die . . . '

'You did your guardian angel bit.'

'It's a business arrangement, Luke, not an act of charity. My expenses will be reflected in my final account.'

'We're not there yet, are we?' Luke said, his remaining bruises standing out more than ever against the pale flesh of his face. In that moment, Tania's courage almost failed her. The hell of it all was that, despite everything, she still loved him. She always would. Why wasn't it possible to love to order? Why, when it hit you, did it come like a bolt out the blue? And with someone every fibre of your body tells you shouldn't love?

'We never will be, Luke.' A simple sentence had never before cost her so much personal emotion. She gripped the sheet. There would be no going back.

She recoiled from the light of anger now in Luke's eyes. 'You can't do this. We had an agreement . . . '

'A professional one.'

'It sure doesn't seem particularly professional at this moment, or do you always conduct your business meetings in bed?'

Tania struggled with the sheets, unable to breathe. She had to get up, get out, go anywhere but here. Incapacitated as he was, Luke anchored her body to his by rolling over on top of her. 'Answer me.' He shook her arms, beads of sweat moistening his forehead. Tania could taste salt on her lips, the salt of his sweat.

'Luke.' He was having difficulty breathing. She could hear the rasping draw deep in his lungs, 'For goodness sake.' He was breathing harshly now as he struggled to speak.

'And what about that business on the floor? Is that an optional extra too? Do you offer it as a professional service to all your customers?'

'Stop it, Luke. You'll have a relapse.'

'You're not disappearing out my life again. You've got a job to do here, and do it you damned well will.'

'I never said I wouldn't complete . . . '

'There's at least six months' work and, when we get to the end of that, I'll think of another six months' work.'

'We're on a time penalty clause.'

'Open to renegotiation. You should read the small print.'

Had she signed a contract? Tania couldn't remember. She was normally so careful, but there'd been so much paperwork, it was possible it had slipped through — but how? She was too blindingly tired to work it out.

'You can't do this to me.' Panic filled her words.

'Can't I?' His words had a hollow ring of authenticity. 'How do you think I got where I am today? I don't do things by the book. Surely you realise that by now? I do things *my* way. And I get results.'

'I'll sue.' She didn't want to believe him, but his words held the certainty of truth.

'Try that and I'll drag your name through every court in the country. By the time I've finished with you, there won't be a person left in the land who won't have heard of you and what you get up to on the floors of your client's houses. There won't be anyone left who'd dream of giving you a commission. You'd be finished. You needn't bother fighting with the sheets. I'm going.' He flung her back on to the mattress in disgust. His parting shot was 'And don't even think of disappearing. I'll find you wherever you go.'

Tania curled over in a foetal ball and listened to Luke cursing himself into his clothes. She now had the proof she'd been looking for. Beyond a shadow of doubt, Luke Sinclair was capable of sidelining anyone who got in his way. He'd done it to Harry . . . and now he was doing it to her!

She heard the scrape of his crutches as he struggled down the stairs. The front door banged to. Then there was the most total silence Tania had ever known in her whole life.

14

How Tania got through the next few days, she had no idea. In fact, she could only put it down to gritty determination — that Luke Sinclair would not get the better of her. She'd make this the best job she'd ever done, and the results would speak for themselves. They'd be the advertisement for her professionalism, not any mud-slinging campaign orchestrated by Luke.

Ignoring the sly smiles of one or two of the workmen the next morning, she'd carried on with her commission, leading by example, the first to arrive in the morning and the last to leave at night. This was the hands-on part about her job that she really enjoyed — getting down to the basics, rubbing up old wood, experimenting with colour schemes, painting sections of wall to see if her ideas would work. And then the final magic moment when they did, when it all came together like a jigsaw puzzle. She'd never felt so stimulated by a project — or so dead emotionally.

Tania had made sure Luke's fleeting visits to the house had coincided with her absences — apart from one unfortunate incident. She picked up on builder gossip that his business empire was having a few troubles and his time was tied up jetting back and forth to the States. That situation suited her fine.

She'd had to hide a smile of satisfaction when, hearing his voice down a corridor unexpectedly one morning and concealing herself behind a convenient wall-screen in one of the bedrooms, she'd heard him complaining that life was more difficult now he couldn't fly Concorde across the Atlantic.

'My heart bleeds for you,' she hadn't been able to stop herself from retorting, then realised to her double horror that she'd spoken out loud and that Luke and the builder were actually in the same room. Through the fine weave of the screen, she could feel Luke's eyes mockingly turned in her direction and knew he'd seen her, probably even known she'd been there all the time. Why did she act so out of character whenever he was around?

She blushed as she heard him discussing the strength of the flooring with the foreman and wanting to know exactly how much activity it would support. He was doing it on purpose, she thought, not wanting to, but not being able to stop herself, remembering the night he'd arrived on crutches and fallen at her feet. To her relief, she heard footsteps leaving the room. She crept out from behind the screen just as Luke strolled back in. Frozen to the spot, Tania watched him cross the room in an agony of embarrassment.

'Good morning,' he greeted her with a deceptively civil smile, 'left my briefcase somewhere. Ah, here it is.' He picked it up and headed towards the door. Tania's relief was short-lived. He turned back to her. 'Tell me,' he asked. 'Is this some new age way of working? Some 'behind the screen' thing?' His smile invited her to share the pun, but Tania was in no mood for sharing anything with Luke Sinclair. She never wanted to see him again, she had to keep reminding herself, despite the fact her heart was singing at the sight of him. 'Don't you dare,' the amusement had drained from his face as, goaded beyond endurance, Tania had lifted a wet paintbrush-loaded hand. She would have flung it at him if he hadn't decided discretion was the better part of valour and made a hurried and somewhat undignified exit from the room.

Tania had booked herself a permanent room at The Feathers but, some nights, she didn't even get back there to sleep. Under her guidance and innovation, she could feel the fabric of the house coming alive. If only it hadn't been for Luke Sinclair, everything would have been perfect.

'You'll wear yourself out, Miss

Jordan, if you don't mind my saying so,' the security guard said when he came on duty one evening. 'Have you eaten anything today?'

Her eyes were as bruised as Luke's had been after his accident as she brushed paint-stained hair out of her eyes. She just couldn't get the right shade of oak stain for the fine quality wainscoting. It had to be absolutely right. She was not giving Luke Sinclair one reason to fault her work. Then, when it was all finished, she'd call his bluff and leave. She wouldn't be held to ransom.

'Here,' the guard thrust a foil packet into her hands. Tania looked at it, not sure what she was supposed to do. 'Eat,' he urged unwrapping the sandwiches. 'Cheese and tomato — protein to build you up. My wife always makes enough for two.'

The sight of food churned Tania's stomach, but she forced herself to swallow a few bites and sip some of his scalding tea.

'Thank you,' she remembered to say with a wan smile.

'You'll make yourself ill,' the guard chided as he leaned forward and looked into her face with concern.

'So this is how you spend your time.' A third voice sliced between them making them jump.

The security guard swore as he spilt his tea. Tania let his sandwiches slip from her lap unnoticed. Luke stood in the doorway, blue eyes absorbing the scene. 'Very cosy.' Now his bruises had faded and his crutches been confined to a cupboard, he was back to his old self — as heart wrenchingly handsome as ever. Tania's stomach did its usual trapeze act on her insides. If the guard hadn't been there as a buffer, she'd have screamed at Luke to go away and leave her alone.

Why did it have to be like this? Why hadn't he been honest with her? If he had inadvertently caused Harry's accident, why wouldn't he tell her about it? Why couldn't he set her free to love him?

'Just sharing a snack, sir.' The guard shuffled to his feet in embarrassment. 'I'll do my rounds, shall I?' He made a hurried getaway before Tania had the presence of mind to call him back. The last thing she wanted was to be alone with Luke Sinclair.

Luke ambled into the room. Tania noticed he was wearing another of his floral ties — a huge tiger lily, bright orange on a green background. It clashed horribly with his quiet grey business suit and pale-blue shirt. She supposed that when you ran the show, you could get away with anything — even ties as outrageous as his. They'd planted a tiger lily together, she remembered, their first day. He'd promised to bring her a bud of it, but she'd watched it bud, bloom and die, like their relationship.

'Hello Luke,' she said, hoping this meeting wasn't going to result in another soul-destroying confrontation.

He sat down on the upturned orange

box recently vacated by the security guard.

'You don't really want these do you?' he asked gently, rewrapping the sandwiches in their foil and placing them carefully next to the guard's flask. He screwed the top back on. 'He'll need that later,' he said by way of explanation, 'Gets pretty lonely here in the middle of the night. But you know all about that, don't you? Remember? When you bopped me on the head because you thought I was an intruder? Seems like years ago, doesn't it?'

Tania didn't like this gentle, thoughtful Luke, looking after the security guard's flask and midnight snack, reminiscing on their past misdeeds. She didn't trust him. He was at his most dangerous when he was nice. She wanted to be able to shout at him, accuse him of being a heartless beast, not sitting on an upturned orange box, reminding her of the man she thought she had fallen in love with — a man who didn't exist.

Something twisted inside Luke's stomach as he took in the enormous eyes, shadowed by fatigue, and wary as an animal's trapped in a car's head-lights. This wasn't how he had meant it to be. Tania was supposed to have fallen in love with him and, happy ever after, they were to have done up The Peacock House together — the gardener's stepson and the daily's daughter. Only it hadn't turned out to be the modern fairytale of his dreams. Tania was looking at him now as if she loathed him and there was nothing he could do about it. She thought he was respon-sible for Harry's accident. He could see it in her eyes. What hope did he have when the woman he would die for thought he had caused the death of her first love, then drove away from the scene and fled to another country? He hadn't dared tell her the truth, and now it was too late. Because he hadn't told her, she'd assumed the rumours associ-ating him with the accident were true. His silence had been his condemnation.

'Don't you ever sleep?' he asked.

Tania blinked herself back to the present. Her thoughts, had she but known it, had been on a parallel with Luke's. 'The job needs to be done . . . '

'Not at the expense of your health. Have you looked in the mirror lately?'

'Mirror?' Tania repeated the word as if she didn't understand it. 'No I don't think I have.'

'You've lost weight, your hair's like a bird's nest and there are dark circles under your eyes.'

'Whose fault is that?' she stung back at him.

Luke hid a wry smile. That was more like his spirited Tania. She wasn't made for this self-flagellation bit. She was feisty, independent, ready to shout back at him. He loved her so much he had a permanent pain in his groin just thinking about her.

'If it's any consolation, I think you're doing a wonderful job. All the men on the premises seem to be half-in-love with you. The foreman's got nothing but praise for you. The men are all in awe of you and that security guard brings in extra sandwiches with his tea, just to make sure you eat something.'

Tania looked down at the thermos lid of tea she was still holding. It had grown cold. She put it down with a small sigh.

'Hardly the reaction I was expecting,' Luke said, a pained look on his face.

'Did you expect me to go down on my knees in gratitude?'

'No,' Luke conceded. 'I didn't expect you to go quite that far, but . . . '

'It's been the hardest work I've ever done in my life. The builders are here as soon as it gets light. They've worked their butts off and for what? So some rich cyber-geek can enjoy the spoils of their labour from his ill gotten gains.'

Luke shifted on his orange box. 'That's a pretty comprehensive character assassination. I'm not sure I agree with all the . . . '

'Then add to it the list of things you're going to sue me for.'

A shy night breeze wafted through the open windows as if it wasn't sure it would be welcome. Tania closed her eyes, grateful for its freshness, but uncertain she had the energy to open them again.

'You don't mean that, do you?' Luke asked.

'Don't mean what?' she asked, stretching the back of her neck with her eyes still closed.

'Want a massage?'

If Luke so much as put one finger on her flesh . . .

'No,' she jolted upright, peeling open her eyes. 'Just a bit tired, that's all.'

'Liar. You're exhausted.' Luke reminded her of a panther, stalking her every move ready to pounce at the slightest hesitation.

'If I am exhausted, it's because I'm fighting to fulfil every last sentence of your crippling penalty clause and, in answer to your question, I meant every word of what I said. The work we've all done here is brilliant. We've put our heart into it and it shows. And I also meant every word I said about you, and you can go ahead and sue me.' There was a responsive flash of emotion in Luke's eyes and Tania tensed, ready for the sparks to fly.

'You know I don't want to do that, Tania.'

'Don't do this to me, Luke. You've played on my emotions enough. I'm immune to whatever it is you're offering.'

Luke felt the ring box in his trouser pocket and turned his eyes away from the fire in Tania's. He didn't know why he kept carrying it around with him. He supposed in one small corner of his heart, he nurtured a faint flicker of hope like an eternal flame.

'I'm just so sorry that you and I . . . ' Tania drank some of the guard's tea — it was stone cold by now, but she gulped it down, desperate to ease the dryness in her throat before she continued, 'couldn't make it together.'

Luke's face tightened, whitening the

hairline scar on his cheek. 'Tania . . . '

She backed away from his out-stretched hand. 'Don't touch me.'

Luke immediately retracted, ice in his eyes. 'Do I repel you that much?'

A reluctant smile moved Tania's lips. 'I'm covered in oak stain. You don't want to get it on your suit or that tie, although the colour might improve it.' She knew she was being inane, but she couldn't think straight. Just being this close to Luke was making her dizzy! Would she ever be free of the spell he seemed to be casting over her? She looked him up and down. 'Aren't you a little overdressed for visiting the work-site? Wouldn't a borrowed shirt and jeans be better?'

'Only if they're one size too big,' he said in such a low voice that Tania had to lean forward to catch his words. He was looking at her now with such an expression on his face that, had she been able to, Tania would have given herself to him there and then, but he didn't follow it up. Instead he said, in a return to his normal voice, 'I'm dressed like this because I came to see how you were getting on before I go back to the States. And that's not a free licence for you to disappear again. I've only just got the Harley back and the insurance wouldn't stand another accident. Or me come to that. I've still got a bit of a bump on the back of my head. Since meeting you, I've become a mass of bumps and bruises.'

'You're going back? For how long?'

'I don't know. The partner I was handing over to has health problems. I need to get it all straight before I head back.' He leaned forward, his tiger lily tie swinging gently backward and forward, the vivid colours hypnotising Tania. 'Promise you'll stay?'

'I promise,' Tania said, unable to believe her body could let her down at a time like this and after all she had gone through with Luke. Despite everything, knowing him for the coward he was, she'd walk barefoot over hot coals just to have him smile at her and beg her not to leave. Her lip curled in disgust with herself. How could she be so spineless to even think such things?

'Don't . . . Tania . . . '

'What?'

'Look at me like that.'

'Like what?'

'As if you loathe me.'

'Loathe you?' She broke into an unnatural laugh. 'Loathe you?' She hiccuped. 'You still don't understand, do you?'

'Don't understand what?'

'I don't loathe you. I . . . '

'Yes?'

There was a noise on the gravel outside. Luke swore under his breath as Tania froze. She'd been about to confess that she loved him. Lack of food was obviously making her light-headed. She hated him!

'There's someone outside,' she said, reducing her voice to a whisper. Whoever it was would have heard every word.

'Only my driver. Tania,' he said,

urgency driving his words, 'What were you about to say? Just now? I have to know.'

'I . . . don't remember,' she finished faintly. 'Luke, I have to get on and you have a flight to catch. No,' her voice rose to a higher pitch, 'don't touch me.' If he did, she'd surrender everything . . . her values, her self-respect, her hatred of him. As long as they stayed apart, she could just about manage to get through this farce of a commission.

'Am I so very abhorrent to you?' His jaw was so stiff he could hardly speak.

'Just go, Luke, please,' she implored him. 'I'll be here when you get back. We've about another three months to completion.'

'And then . . . ?'

She raised her storm-driven eyes to his. 'I don't know.'

'I'll never let you go,' he said as a discreet cough outside reminded them they weren't alone. 'What?' Luke spun around to face the invisible throat clearer.

A figure moved forward out the shadows. 'Excuse me, sir. If you want to make the early flight, we ought to be leaving now. There's traffic hold-ups on the motorway and check-in is at least two hours before departure.'

'Yes, all right. Go and start the car.'

'Promise me . . . ' Luke grabbed the sleeve of Tania's work shirt. There was none of the big hitting tycoon about him now! 'Promise me you'll be here when I get back.' He seemed to struggle with his next words. 'I . . . the rumours . . . about me . . . Harry's accident . . . '

Tania heard the purr of Luke's car as the driver brought it up to the front of the house.

'Yes?'

'Look,' he glanced at his watch and swore, 'Wait for me. I'll tell you when I get back, I promise. Only, don't believe everything you hear or read about it.'

'Why didn't you tell me before?'

'When you've kept quiet about something for so long, it's difficult to break the habit. I wanted you to believe in me, believe that I wouldn't do such a thing. I wanted to tell you in my own time what really happened.'

Wave after wave of shame swept over Tania. She had believed the rumours — unequivocally. But Luke hadn't exactly encouraged her to doubt them.

'Wait for me?'

Tania nodded. 'I'll be here.'

Luke raised a hand to her face and tweaked one of her curls playfully.

'Sir?' a voice interrupted them.

'That man,' he said barely moving his lips, 'is the only thing that stands between you, me, and the floor.'

The room rotated around Tania. Lack of food and the nearness of Luke's body to hers were too much for her food-and-sleep deprived system. Also, she wasn't too sure she'd understood Luke.

'You mean here? On the floor? What . . . ?'

'I mean here,' Luck acknowledged gravely, 'on the floor. And on that note, I think I'd better go before I get us both into more trouble.'

He hadn't touched her, but her skin was flooded with fire.

Tania stayed where she was long after his car had disappeared down the drive, long after the guard had completed his tour of the upstairs rooms and locked the downstairs ones. Suddenly, she wasn't tired any more.

Energised, she watched the sun rise on the new month — July — and listened to the early morning noises of the garden. On stiffened legs, she walked slowly out on to the patio and over the dew-dropped grass to the kitchen garden. The door was very stiff, but it yielded to her pressure. This was where it had all begun.

It had been the middle Saturday of Wimbledon and her mother had been glued to the tennis. Unable to stay indoors, Tania had walked through the village to The Peacock House, scrambled through one of the back hedges and, with brambles in her hair and scratches on her knees, lay in the grass and popped gooseberry after gooseberry into her mouth. Mr Harrison had found her and told her to stay hidden while old Lady Fitzroy, Harry's grandmother, did her rounds. Giggling with nerves, she'd buried herself in the long grass and moments later Luke had joined her, banished too from the imposing presence of the Dowager Lady Fitzroy. There they'd crammed more gooseberries into their mouths, and Luke had put his arm round her shoulders and told her to duck down as Lady Fitzroy swept past them. She had come so close to them that her long thin shoes had flicked grass cuttings in Tania's face. Luke had smothered his laughter when she'd come up for air, choking on grass and gooseberry, and wiped the juice from her lips and picked the brambles out of her hair.

How could she have forgotten? If she closed her eyes, she could smell the gooseberries now, feel their prickly skins, hear the peacocks wailing, feel the sun on her bare legs. Were the ghosts of the past always so evocative?

She closed the door slowly. She needed a shower and a shot of caffeine. It was too early to descend on The Feathers. Crossing the lawn, she headed towards The Lodge. There was a downstairs shower. She didn't need to go upstairs, didn't need to see the room where she and Luke had . . .

She let the lukewarm water trickle over her tiredness and wash the dust and paint stains off her skin and out of her hair. Rinsing her underwear, she pegged it out on the line. The heat from the sun was already warm enough to dry it.

She strolled back into the kitchen humming to herself. A shadow moved forwards from the hallway and Tania dropped her mug to the floor in shock.

'Who's there?'

'You just can't stay away can you?'

Tania smelt Jasmine. It choked the back of her throat. She swayed.

'What are you doing here?'

'I could ask you the same question.'

Shuna emerged from the shadows of the hall. She was wearing one of her shot silk dresses and the material strained over her stomach. Shuna was, by anybody's calculations, several months pregnant. Luke had lied to her again!

15

An autumn haze shimmered over the long meadow grass, damp from the early morning dew. Tania's eyes hurt from the violence of the achingly blue sky. Soon she would leave and this time she would never come back. She'd fulfilled her contract and there was nothing else to keep her here. Why then did nature have to throw the full works at her? She took a deep breath and closed her eyes. Apples, wood smoke, wet leaves, and that special tang that epitomises an English autumn — crisply sharp and a heart-wrenching *aide-mémoir* of all she was about to lose.

With a calm dignity that she was far from feeling, she turned back to the house. Burnt sienna brick with golden highlights smiled back at her. Ferrous sulphate-coloured lace hydrangeas dipped their heavy heads in the early morning shade, not quite ready to raise their full glory to the strength of the sun.

Tania's foot came into contact with several spiky burrs underneath the horse chestnut tree. She picked one up and drew off the flesh revealing a shiny brown conker inside. It was smooth and wet against her fingertips. She stroked it, grateful for the calming therapy of an inanimate object.

She'd seen a slash of red Ferrari through the trees a few moments ago. Luke had come back. Her throat felt as prickly as the conker but at the prospect of seeing him again — for the last time. It had been difficult keeping up the pretence of normality over the telephone, but she had the excuse of a poor transatlantic connection to blame for any oddness in her voice. Luke had kept her posted daily either by email or a telephone call on the situation in the States. Hal was being given early retirement and a brash American executive was taking his place.

'Soon be home,' he'd said during their last telephone call. 'We'll have a housewarming party once things are sorted out. When do you think — Christmas, New Year? Spring's a good time. We can stay up all night and watch the sunrise. You decide.'

He'd sounded so full of plans and Tania had tried to go along with them, knowing deep down that nothing would come of them. She wouldn't be here. But she wouldn't run away again, like she had once before. He deserved being told to his face why she was leaving.

And now Luke was back. Tania needed a few quiet moments to herself to prepare her goodbye. She shivered and let the conker slip from her fingers. She'd done loads of dress rehearsals in her mind, but now she couldn't remember one of them.

Shuna could have been lying about the baby being Luke's. Tania knew that but, whatever the truth, there was no future for Tania at The Peacock House.

Most of the gaps in her past had been filled now, but the biggest one to be breached was the one between herself and Luke.

She wiped mud and grass off her leather shoes, careful not to scuff them. She mustn't get it wrong today. Her business suit was professional and her hair firmly in place. There must be no slip-ups or undignified behaviour. She meant business and needed the armour of her uniform to protect her. The Tania Jordan who wore old shirts and let her hair hang loose had no place in today's action. Today was big business, possibly the biggest of her career, and she was dressed for it!

Luke's car was parked outside the oak door. The engine was still cooling down and making clicking noises, reminding Tania of the time bomb about to explode between them.

She glanced towards The Lodge where her own car was packed and waiting. It was facing the wrought-iron gates ready for the quick departure

Tania envisaged. He'd left them open and she was glad now that they'd decided not to go for electronically operated ones. Renovated by the original workman who still lived in the village and who'd been delighted to restore them at his own leisurely pace, they'd been returned to their traditional state, even to the extent of using the same shade of weather paint as the original. It had been the small details like this that had made the job so worthwhile. Luke had been generous on budget and Tania, who'd made it a point of ethics to work within his guidelines, had never felt so professionally fulfilled. It would be a serious blow to return to the petty squabbling she was used to encountering in her work. In fact, life in general was going to be so much duller . . . without Luke.

And Luke was waiting for her now in The Peacock House. And she'd come to say good-bye. Tania lingered a second, watching him as he looked round the redecorated entrance hall, absorbing the beauty and fine-crafted woodwork of the original oak. The end result more than justified the hours of work she'd put into tracking down exactly the right shade of stain to use, to preserve the heritage and beauty of the beams and the solid staircase. A hint of beeswax scented the motes of dust dancing in the morning sunbeams streaming through the pane glass windows, now polished to a diamond sparkle.

Tania's breath caught in her throat at the unspoilt beauty and, hearing her behind him, Luke turned, smiled, and held out his arms. Tania hesitated on the threshold fighting down the urge to run into his arms, feel them lock round her body, tight in an embrace secure from all demons. But there was no embrace strong enough to destroy the demons between herself and Luke.

'I was just coming to find you,' he said, still limping slightly. 'Tania?' Tania tried to walk towards him, but she needed the doorjamb for support.

Where've you been?' A small frown rearranged the scar on the bridge of Luke's nose. It would heal in time, thought Tania. Physical scars did — it was the mental ones that never left you.

'Hello Luke. You're looking better.' She forced herself to smile, 'Less of a crock than when I last saw you.'

And that, thought Tania, was the understatement of the century. He looked jaw-droppingly gorgeous — not conventionally handsome, of course, but then nothing about Luke Sinclair was ever conventional. Her memory did another flash as more pieces of the jigsaw of her past fell into place.

How could she have fallen in love with Harry Fitzroy and not remembered Luke? A dagger turned in her heart. She so wanted to love him, faults and all. She did love him, but the past would always be there to haunt them. A past he hadn't invited her to share, which more than screamed his guilt. If only he'd been open with her from the beginning, she would have understood.

But he hadn't. He'd shut her out.

Luke's eyes moved from hers to the business blue of her suit and his smile faltered.

'You look very formal.' His voice too held question.

'I thought it appropriate — for a business meeting and the dissolving of a partnership.'

The frown lines on his forehead deepened and the Michaelmas daisy tie creased as Luke took a lunging step towards her. If Tania hadn't known better, she'd have sensed panic in the action, like that of a drowning man. But panic wasn't on the agenda, although turning and running could be an option if things got — difficult.

'What are you talking about?' he demanded. 'What business meeting? Partnership?'

'I have a check list here.' Tania had grabbed her briefcase off the oak-backed seat by the door, and she clutched it to her like a shield as she recoiled from the colour of Luke's eyes.

They were angry black. 'And I need to return your keys,' she continued. 'Perhaps a signature?'

Luke went so pale that Tania could detect the faint stains of the bruises he'd sustained in his accident. She swallowed. She really didn't want to hurt him. She wasn't out for revenge — just a quick, clean getaway.

'What's happened?'

'We've finished. Haven't you noticed? I just need to go through one or two things with you, explain . . . '

Luke snatched the clipboard from Tania's trembling hands with such force he tore one of her manicured finger-nails. She winced.

'I don't like your nails like that,' he grabbed her hand and dragged her to him, 'Or your hair up like that.' With a movement so swift that Tania couldn't react, he tweaked her anchor hairpin and it fell to the floor in a scatter of subsidiary pins as her elaborate hair-do collapsed. Luke mussed the dislodged mane of hair, shiny as the conker she'd discarded, and then gripped it with such savagery that Tania whimpered.

'What's this all about?'

'No, don't. Luke. Please.' She closed her eyes and staggered backwards. But Luke didn't let go and Tania whimpered as, by the same crude method, he yanked her body back into his arms.

'You're not getting away, so don't even try to escape.'

To her horror, Tania could feel her body responding to his. She hadn't seen Luke for two months, two months of torture when she'd put herself on a treadmill of hard labour. Two months during which she hadn't given herself time to think about Shuna, babies, Luke, or her future — two barren months when no physical emotion had been allowed to touch her. And her body was letting her know it was hungry, starved of needs only Luke could satisfy.

But he didn't feel the same about her. He couldn't.

'I don't know what Luke's told you,

but the baby is his.' Tania could hear Shuna's soft voice that day at The Lodge, the morning of the last day she'd seen Luke.

And then, further back in time, in Ellie's garden.

'There were rumours when Harry died — a motorbike — a Harley-Davidson . . . it left the scene without reporting the accident according to the *Gazette*.'

A vivid stripe of orange and yellow streaked through the shards of Tania's memory, together with night rides under the stars and the smell of hot leather. Even that had been a sham. He'd done it before — with Shuna.

'He loved that bike,' Shuna had said. 'Sometimes, I think, more than he loved me. We did our courting on it. He used to take me for moonlit spins through the villages, along the river, out into the country. We made love once, under the stars. I hope you don't love Luke too much, Tania. He won't be faithful to you.'

'I don't love him at all,' Tania had lied.

And ever since that day, she'd been trying to convince herself it was the truth.

'Let me go, Luke,' she whispered.

'Never,' his voice was as hoarse as hers had been. 'You're mine. I've waited ten years for this moment and I'm not giving up now.'

Tania stumbled from the pressure of Luke's body against hers.

'You can take me to court, blacken my professional integrity, whatever. But you can't force me to stay.'

Luke's fingertips made cruel dents in the soft flesh of her neck.

'Did you really think I meant what I said? I could never have done that. I just couldn't think of any other way to keep you. I'm no good with words, Tania, but you're my life. You can't walk out on me.'

Tania clung to him as shocks sped through her body. She dared not open her eyes, scared to identify the origin of the patter of buttons falling to the floor. Luke's cold hand on her warm breast provided the answer. In one movement, he'd ripped open her blouse. A bubble of panic rose in her throat. Perhaps he'd stop if she didn't respond.

'Tania, don't do this to me.' His voice came from the region of her midriff. She could feel his fingers tugging at her skirt button.

'No.' Inertia wasn't working. She had to do something — stop him before she too lost control and her body's appetites took over.

With a superhuman strength she didn't know she possessed, Tania pushed and separated her body from Luke's, crossing her hands over the exposed top half of her body in a protective gesture of defence. Her breath came in short, sharp gasps of pain. Moisture oozed from every pore. What remained of her blouse stuck to her flesh.

Like a puppet operated by strings he couldn't control, Luke jerked away from her, his shoes cracking over the scattered blouse buttons.

'Tania?' There was a glaze of sweat on his forehead and his eyes were as blue as the autumn sky outside and as hypnotic. 'For heaven's sake, tell me what is going on. Has Shuna been making more trouble? Is that it?'

'I need you to tell me,' the words tumbled from Tania's lips.

'Tell you what?'

The cauldron bubbling up inside Tania boiled over.

'The truth.' She hurled at him. 'What really happened when Harry died?'

'I've never lied to you.'

'Everything you've told me has been based on deceit. Your whole life has been built on a fabrication of false-hoods.'

'Tania, whatever I've done, or what you think I've done, has only been for you.' For a nano-second Tania blacked out.

'You admit it?' There it was — in the cold light of day — the truth at last.

362

'I bought this house for you because we both loved it. Remember?'

Tania realised she had been clutching the keys in her hand. The sharpness of the shanks had even drawn blood. She wiped her hand numbly down her blouse, streaking the pristine white cotton with a vivid smear of red.

'Here,' she held them out to him. When he didn't take them, she bent down and slowly placed them on the floor.

'They're yours.'

Tania had never heard such sadness in his voice.

'I don't want them. I want nothing from you,' she said.

'Why? Don't you realise I love you? I've always loved you, you have to believe me. What else do I have to do to convince you?'

Bitterness backed up in Tania's throat. She loved him too, that was the Greek tragedy of the affair.

'I could never love a man who deserted his pregnant ex-wife . . . '

'Bloody hell.' Luke swore roundly. 'You know Shuna's economical with the truth, I've told you that. She'll say anything to get what she wants.'

'I've seen her, Luke. She is pregnant. You said she wasn't.'

'It doesn't matter. The baby's not mine. Do you really think I'd leave her if it were? What type of person do you take me for?'

'And Harry? What about him?' Around them, the morning went still as Tania ploughed on. 'Can you deny you were drinking with him the night he died?'

'No. I'm not . . . '

'Or that you deserted him as his car crashed into . . . ' Tania's voice cracked. She couldn't go on.

Luke froze in front of her. His flesh seemed to disappear, stripped off his bones until he almost resembled a skeleton.

'No.'

With his acceptance of her accusation, the last vestiges of hope died in her. Even if Harry had been drinking too much and been unfaithful to her, he didn't deserve to be abandoned by the roadside to die. Tania couldn't think of how many other lives had been affected by the callous indifference of the man standing in front of her.

'You believe I'm guilty, don't you? Say it.'

'I . . . I . . . '

'It's your eyes. They always give you away.' She could hear the destroying disappointment of defeat in Luke's voice now. 'You're right. If you think like that, there is clearly no future for us together.'

'Don't.' Tania grabbed her bag, but Luke was too quick for her.

'No, I won't let you go. You've had your say. It's time for me to have mine.'

'It's too late . . . '

'I didn't tell you what happened that night . . . ' Luke took a deep breath, 'for personal reasons.'

'I can guess . . . '

'No. You can't.' Luke put up a gentle

hand to stroke her face. 'Then I hoped, after you'd found out I was there from Ellie, that you'd believe I wouldn't have driven off leaving Harry to . . . ' Luke stopped unable to go on.

'I don't . . . '

'Only a rat would desert a sinking ship.' Luke had started to speak again. 'And you think I'm just such a rat.'

'What choice have you given me? You wouldn't tell me your side of the story. What was I to believe? You shut me out — why? You talk about trust but you didn't trust me.'

'I didn't tell you because I was hoping it wouldn't be necessary. Because I was hoping that, one day, you'd come to love me as much as I love you — without condition. But it was always Harry, wasn't it? You didn't even remember me. I thought perhaps I'd been given another chance when this house came on the market and I managed to work Ellie into offering your services. Well, I know better now, don't I? For what it's worth, I didn't desert Harry that night. But then I don't expect you to believe me. You don't, do you? Look at me, Tania.' Her head had fallen forward, but the compulsion in his voice raised her eyes to his.

'Not like that,' he ground at her, 'not with eyes that can see only what they want to see.'

'Please, Luke. Just let me go. Everything's been completed within the time penalty.'

'You're not going — yet. I haven't finished.'

'I don't want to listen.'

'Until I've explained about Harry.'

'It's too late.'

'You mean you've already made up your mind?'

'I mean, I don't want to listen to more half-truths, twisted facts. Luke, I'm tired. I've been working eighteen-hour days for weeks now. I just want to go home and sleep.'

The fight seemed to sag out of Luke. 'If that's what you really want,' he bowed his head.

Tania began doing up the remaining buttons on her blouse.

'Not like that,' Luke said gently, slapping her hands apart with his. Tania's chest heaved against his hands as she fought to control her breath. Very carefully he undid the buttons. 'You've got them in the wrong holes,' he said, his fingers skimming her flesh as he refastened them correctly. 'There. The others are on the floor so, unless you have a needle and thread, that's the best I can do.'

'Thank you.'

'So? Paperwork?' he said, still in the same tender tone of voice.

Tania looked round. She couldn't remember what she'd done with the clipboard. Luke picked it up off the chair, and flipped through Tania's copious notes.

'I'm sure it's all in order,' he said. 'I'll look through it properly and send you a signed copy within the next few days.'

Tania's eyes felt hot but she was

shivering. Pinpricks of doubt punctured her conscience. She hadn't given Luke a proper chance to explain. He'd wanted to wait and tell her in his own time. Had she got everything totally wrong? She was too drained to know, or care.

A beam of sunlight picked out the keys still on the floor between them. Luke knelt down slowly and picked them up. His lips moved in a smile of such incredible sadness and disappointment that Tania wanted to rush into his arms, give him one more chance. But it was too late. They'd been travelling at the wrong speed and in the wrong direction.

Luke had said he'd always loved her. She still couldn't remember everything. Why? Was it because she didn't want to remember what she feared . . . that Luke was guilty? Or had she condemned him because she didn't trust herself to love him? Was it some sort of blunted shock reaction to Harry?

'Would it be totally out of order to

kiss you one last time?' Tania blinked the sun out of her eyes. This was too much. 'I promise I won't be a nuisance.' He smiled, his finger stroking her chin gently. 'Or give you a rotten press — if you let me kiss you.'

'That's blackmail.'

'Yes, it is.'

If Luke hadn't been supporting her chin, her head would have fallen forward in a gesture of defeat. She had no ammunition left to battle with. But Luke Sinclair wasn't going to fight. He was going out of her life — forever.

The touch of his lips on hers was hesitant, then firmer. Tania closed her eyes, wanting this moment to last a lifetime. Then, with the impact of shock therapy, the final piece of the jigsaw slotted into place. Luke had given her her first grown-up kiss, after a party at the Fitzroys. Harry had been flirting outrageously with — she couldn't remember the girl's name now — but Tania had escaped to the terrace and was watching the peacocks silhouetted in the evening light, pretending with all the bravado of youth that she wasn't upset. It had been a summer party. The Fitzroys had one every July and they invited all Harry's set. There'd been some high-flyers, girls with aristocratic double-barrelled names and boys driving fast cars. Had Tania realised then she had no place in their world? From different directions, she and Luke had both drifted to the same refuge. She remembered he'd put an arm round her shoulders and turned her towards him.

'What am I doing to do?' she'd whispered.

'When you're old enough, I'll come with a sapphire ring, the colour of your eyes, and propose to you. Will you accept me?'

She'd laughed lightly, let him kiss her, and not taken the words seriously — until now.

'It's all right,' he said soothingly, following her train of thought. 'I won't hold you to an adolescent promise.'

'Promise?'

Luke smiled and felt in his pocket. 'Take it. No strings attached. I'd like you to have it.'

He produced a blue box and opened it carefully before putting it into Tania's shaking hand. Nestling inside was a sapphire ring — Victorian — in a marquise setting of pointed oval.

'The colour reminded me of the peacocks and your eyes,' he said.

'I can't take it, Luke.'

'Wear it sometimes and think of me.' He gave a slow sad smile. 'Goodbye.'

Tania didn't realise he had gone until she heard the muted throb of his Ferrari as he eased it down the gravel drive and out through the wrought iron gates. Her hand hurt. She glanced down and saw with puzzled confusion that she was still clutching the ring box. But Luke had gone — she would never see him again.

16

Tania couldn't believe it had been a year. September had disappeared into its own mist, and time had passed in a blur of work and hidden pain.

If she kept working she wouldn't remember and, if she didn't remember, there would be no pain.

And now the daffodils were back, their bright yellow invaded by one rogue magenta tulip smack bang in the middle of Ellie's flowerbed. It unstopped the memory bottle Tania had kept so carefully corked. She remembered — last spring, Ellie's telephone call, and peacocks, and brightly coloured, flower-painted silk ties from Hong Kong . . . and Luke.

'Hey, it says here,' Ellie looked up from her celebrity magazine, that Shuna S has married Xavier. Their baby daughter was an honorary bridesmaid.

Shuna's quoted as stating she's never been so happy in her life. Makes you want to throw up, doesn't it?'

Tania sipped some coffee. She didn't want it, but it eased the aching dryness of her throat. She didn't want to know about Shuna S, her marriage, or her baby, but neither did she want to shout at Ellie to shut up. Without her sister's support over the last few months, she would have gone mad.

Ellie was still avidly reading the article. 'There's no mention of Luke. Still, these interviews always sugar things up don't they? I suppose that they want to make out Shuna's 'Ms Perfect'. But, we know better, don't we?'

Ellie tossed down her magazine and stretched in the sun, slanting her blue eyes at Tania when she thought her sister wasn't looking. 'Thought any more about our little break?' That article about Shuna S might be the godsend Ellie was looking for. She'd got to do something — soon. Tania couldn't go on like this. She'd crack.

Tania dragged her thoughts away from memories and back to Ellie's garden.

'Hmm?' She wasn't sure what Ellie had asked her.

'This weekend. Where d'you fancy going?'

'You choose.'

If Tania hadn't been daydreaming about Luke Sinclair, she'd have noticed the brief glint of triumph in Ellie's eyes. 'Yes,' she hissed under her breath, only just stopping a power salute.

* * *

'Can't imagine why we aren't on the Eurostar.' Ellie made a big deal out of complaining. If she hadn't, she knew Tania would have smelt a big fat rat.

'Your idea,' Tania kept her eyes on the road. She couldn't remember the reason why they'd decided not to go to Paris. Ellie, as usual, had been very organised about the arrangements and

Tania had left her to get on with it. She'd spent half the night making hurried telephone calls, then the other half sitting on the end of Tania's bed giving her a blow-by-blow account of the arrangements she'd made, and what had gone wrong, until Tania hadn't even bothered to listen properly. And that was why she still wasn't exactly sure where they were going. Now Tania came to think about it, Ellie had been secretive about their destination. She should have paid more attention. Ellie had a track record of making Tania do things she didn't want to do — like white water rafting. She hoped this weekend wasn't going to be one of those occasions. She didn't feel up to a disagreement with Ellie. She frowned slightly, a faint shimmer of unease tingling her fingertips. Ellie was up to something. Her body language said 'guilty'.

'Was it? My idea?' Ellie opened her blue eyes in simulated surprise. It hadn't been easy getting Tania to take this break. Contacting Luke and persuading him to fall in with her arrangements had been even more difficult. But Tania didn't know about that — yet. She hoped she wouldn't blow her top when she did.

'You know it was.' A small silence fell between the sisters, before Tania asked, 'So where exactly are we headed for?'

'Er . . . ' Ellie had a huge map spread out on her knees and ducked her head down, making a pretence of studying it. 'Keep going for the moment.'

With a wry glance at Ellie's bowed head, Tania carried on. 'As long as you don't get us hopelessly lost.'

'Would I?' Ellie asked with a show of indignation.

'You would,' Tania allowed a small smile to move her lips. She'd been wrong. Ellie was lost and covering up, that was all. 'I've had experience of your map reading. I remember once . . . '

Ellie let Tania carry on with her

character assassination of her navigational skills. That way she hoped Tania wouldn't notice where they were heading, although it would be a severe test of even her skills to fool Tania all the way to Little Chipping. She hoped by the time she realised what Ellie had planned, it would be too late to turn back. She also hoped Tania would forgive her for interfering. If this worked out, Ellie made a silent promise, she'd never do it again. But she couldn't sit by and watch the person she loved most dearly in the world, after Charles and the boys, destroy herself.

They changed seats just after Great Milton. Ellie took the wheel with shaking hands. She didn't like driving and tended to get lost. It had been years since she'd been to Little Chipping and she wouldn't be able to ask Tania for directions. That really would give the game away.

'Why don't you have a snooze?' she suggested brightly.

The May sunshine was pouring through the open roof of the car and Ellie stifled a yawn, hoping the autosuggestion would work. She knew Tania didn't sleep well and she had kept her awake nearly all last night on purpose. The warm day was a bonus she felt she deserved for all the behind-the-scenes activity, even if it had meant drinking more black coffee than was good for her at the service station. Her own head was feeling a bit fuzzy. As soon as they got to Little Chipping, she was going to leave Luke and Tania to it and get some sleep. Then, later, if they hadn't killed each other — or her — she might suggest dinner with copious amounts of wine. That should do the trick. She crossed her fingers. Even she felt she might have gone over the top on this one!

'Hope you're not going to make a habit of this,' Charles had grumbled as she'd packed him off yet again to his mother's. 'If Tania finds out what you're up to, your life won't be worth living.'

Ellie, for once, had been inclined to agree with Charles, but now with Tania nodding gently in the passenger seat, she knew it had all been worth it. She began to feel a bit more confident. The scheme was going to work. She gave herself a positive pep talk. The only hurdle would be keeping her own eyes open for the rest of the journey.

But it would be worth it, she decided. She'd seen Tania lose weight, working herself to a bag of bones over the winter, insomnia bruises under her eyes, and known she had to do something. Tania wouldn't talk about what had happened between her and Luke, but Ellie decided the missing factor was dialogue. And dialogue meant finding Luke Sinclair and getting him to agree to a meeting. She hadn't been proud of herself going through Tania's briefcase to find her notebook, but there had been no other way. It had taken several telephone calls, including one to an abrasive American female who absolutely refused to put her through, saying Luke was in a meeting or some such excuse. Not to be daunted by such a deterrent and working on the assumption that this was *the* number, Ellie waited until she thought everyone else had gone home and dialled the number again. Luke had answered.

'You won't remember me,' Ellie had started, feeling unbearably nervous. Even now her plans could go pear-shaped.

'On the contrary, I remember you very well . . . and your sister.' His voice sounded flat, a bit like Tania's these days.

Ellie cleared her throat. 'Yes, well, it's her I'm ringing about actually.'

'Nothing's wrong?'

Ellie picked up the quickening of his voice and felt the sniff of success.

'We're going to be in Little Chipping this weekend, and I wondered if you . . . '

'I'll be there.' Luke had disconnected the call leaving Ellie gaping down the line. It was then she absolutely knew that she'd been right.

She frowned as she left the Motorway. This was going to be the tricky bit. If Tania noticed the change in engine note she was done for. But Tania slept on. Holding her breath, Ellie drove carefully through the tourist trap villages, across a tributary of the Leach, and finally into Little Chipping. It was sleeping in the early afternoon sunshine. Ellie held her breath — she'd forgotten how lovely it was. The sun made patterns on the sparkling water, and clumps of late purple crocuses nestled prettily under the village signpost. Even the water trough looked less grey and forbidding in the bright sunshine.

Beside her Tania stirred. Ellie dared not look down. With eyes fixed to the windscreen, she negotiated the road which had turned into a rutted sandy track and kept going.

'Have I slept long?'

Ellie jumped, as Tania stretched out

her long legs then with a yelp, cut short her own languorous sigh. 'Ellie.' She banged her forehead on the windscreen, 'Where are we?' she demanded, frantically rubbing the bump and blinking the tears from her eyes.

'I should have thought that was obvious.'

'What on earth have you done? Turn the car round — now.'

'It's too late, Tania.' Ellie was looking infuriatingly smug. 'Besides I'm dog-tired. I'm going to drop you here and then I'm heading back to The Feathers for some sleep.'

'You're doing no such thing, you interfering . . .'

'Language, Tania,' Ellie grinned, not in the least upset by this sibling outburst. Tania looked more alive than she had done in months. It made a refreshing change. Ellie was fed up to the teeth with having a sister who looked liked the Grim Reaper all the time.

A pleasant faced woman came out of

The Lodge and was busy opening the wrought-iron gates for Ellie to drive through. Tania, still befuddled from her sleep, thought she caught a glimpse of scarlet Ferrari through the trees and exploded again.

'This time you've gone too far, Ellie.'

'How nice to see you both again. I don't suppose you'll remember me, but I knew your mother. Ellie and Tania, isn't it?'

'Yes.' Ellie was out the car. 'You remember Mrs Harrison, don't you Tania? Luke's mother?'

'We'll have tea first,' Mrs Harrison said. 'And then perhaps you'd like to walk down to the house?'

'See you later.'

Ellie had never performed such a neat or quick three-point turn in her life. She left Tania standing, fuming on the driveway outside The Lodge, while Mrs Harrison made polite conversation about the sunshine and how much she'd changed since they'd last seen each other.

Luke was here — at the end of the drive. Tania couldn't think straight. She looked round wildly for an escape route and a weapon to murder Ellie with.

'Darjeeling?' Mrs Harrison hustled Tania inside as if sensing her intentions. 'I don't really like China tea, but I'm sure I could . . . '

Tania tried hard to smile, but her face wouldn't work. 'Indian's fine,' she managed to say. She was never *ever* talking to Ellie again. As far as she was concerned, their relationship was over. If not over, then seriously curtailed. She would not let Ellie interfere in her life again. This latest episode was beyond a joke. Ellie knew Tania's break-up with Luke was a no go area.

'I live here now.' Mrs Harrison bustled round the kitchen. 'Much better than my flat. There's a small garden out the back and I see to the visitors when Luke's not here, take in the post, things like that. I understand the gates were your idea. Much better than electric ones, aren't they? And the house — it's wonderful all the work you did.' She placed a plate of biscuits on the table. Tania looked down at them. And then her eyes strayed to the floor.

It didn't look any different. It was still covered with the same black-and-white cork tiles. Tania felt her colour rising at the memory of her langoustine supper with Luke, a memory which often revisited her in the small hours of the morning when she couldn't sleep.

Mrs Harrison sat down opposite her, poured some tea, urged shortbread on Tania, and then paused for breath.

'Thank you,' Tania gave a weary smile. The tea was welcome, but the biscuit would never get past the blockage in her throat.

'You knew my husband, didn't you? He was the gardener here. He often used to talk about you.'

Tania stirred her tea. This was awful. Unconsciously, Mrs Harrison was tugging at her heartstrings, digging up memories she'd buried in the graveyard of her relationship with Luke.

'Yes.' Tania was unaware how nostalgically soft her voice had grown. 'I do remember.'

'My husband loved it. It's a happy house and garden. It would have broken his heart to leave. Luke knew that too. That's why . . .'

Mrs Harrison stopped speaking and smiled and Tania could see the resemblance to her son. They had the same blue eyes, lively, ready for amusement, kind — but there was no pain in Mrs Harrison's. The last time Tania had seen Luke, his eyes had been deeply filled with pain.

'Yes,' Tania admitted, 'we were all happy.'

'I shouldn't tell you this, but I don't suppose Luke ever will.' Tania stopped stirring her tea.

'I really don't want to talk about . . .'

Mrs Harrison ignored her interruption. 'He kept quiet about the accident . . .'

'Yes, I know.' In a moment Tania would have to get up and leave, manners or no manners.

'For my husband's sake. Only it doesn't matter any more. All the people he could hurt are no longer with us.'

'I'm sorry. I don't . . . '

'It was because of the accident, wasn't it? That you and Luke fell out?'

'I don't . . . '

Mrs Harrison cut her off again. 'One thing I've learned over the years is not to interfere in my son's life, but when Luke rang me to say your sister had contacted him, I knew I had to do something. You see he's got this stupid stiff-necked pride. Sometimes I could bang his head against the nearest wall. Anyway, I got your sister's number from him, and we contrived this little meeting. Were you and Harry Fitzroy close?'

Tania had given up listening. Ellie and Mrs Harrison were two-of-a-kind. She glanced at her watch. If Ellie was at The Feathers, she could make some excuse then get out of here before Luke discovered what her sister and his mother had done. The thought of his being at the end of the drive was spiralling rational thinking out of control.

'I really think I ought to be getting . . . '

Mrs Harrison had gone pink and was fidgeting with the tea cosy on the pot. Tania bit her lip. She hadn't meant to sound so rude. The poor woman was only trying to help, but she was fighting a lost cause. Still, perhaps Tania ought to make an effort to listen.

'Harry was a lovely boy, but a bit weak. There was a rumour about you and him being unofficially engaged. Only, you see, Harry was actually engaged to another girl at the time of his death — the daughter of a friend of his mother's. I think he was plucking up the courage to tell you the night of his accident.'

Robbed of sleep and not having eaten properly for weeks, Tania could feel her system rebelling. If she wasn't careful, she'd slip to the floor. Had she heard correctly?

'We were due to meet up in the pub the night of the accident, but I was late. By the time I got there, they'd all gone.'

'Luke was there with some of his biker friends, having a farewell drink before he went off to America. By the end of the evening, Harry was unsteady on his feet, so Luke drove him home.'

This time the floor really did meet the ceiling as Tania tried to absorb Mrs Harrison's story. 'Luke was driving Harry's car that night?'

'Only as far as the gates to the house. Harry took over. As it was private property from then on, Luke thought he'd be safe. No one knew what really happened after that.'

'What about the race with a motor-bike?'

'That was just a rumour that got out of control. Luke had been seen in the pub that night, but he didn't ride his bike home, one of the others did. That's why there were bike marks on the grass. It was all played down at the request of the Fitzroys. Local people respected them and they were a good family.'

'But it wasn't Luke's fault?'

'No one ever said it was. Luke went up to the house the next day and told them he'd driven as far as the gates. I suppose that's how the rumours started.'

'But Luke's friends, surely they stood by him?'

'None of them knew what really happened and it wouldn't have made any difference. Patti Saunders was packed off to Australia when she came out of hospital and, by that time, Luke had gone off to America. You see, old Lady Fitzroy was very strong on family and didn't want a scandal.'

Tania didn't want to hear about Lady Fitzroy or their supposed family honour. Luke was innocent, yet he'd been branded a tearaway. 'Why didn't Luke protest?'

'Because his stepfather worked for

the Fitzroys. He was a very honourable man, my husband. If there'd been any unpleasantness, he'd probably have felt obliged to give in his notice and Luke wouldn't have wanted him to do anything like that. He loved the house and Luke does too. Like you, he grew up here. The Fitzroys weren't bad people, or wrong. They just thought differently. And Luke loved his stepfather. Mr Harrison was his father in everything but name. Actually Luke did take his name, but he was never officially adopted.'

'And when he went to America he used his real name?' Tania still felt sick. In a roundabout way, Luke had told her all this but she hadn't believed him. She'd thought he'd been covering something up — for all the wrong reasons. He'd been covering up, but only to save the livelihood of his stepfather, a man both she and Luke had loved.

It was all becoming crystal clear now. Luke hadn't told her all the truth out of family loyalty. That was something Tania knew a lot about too. She and Ellie were in the same position. They fought all the time, but there was a fierce loyalty between them, built on trust and love. Tania knew she'd always be there for Ellie, the same way Ellie had poked her nose into Tania's affairs today — out of love. Love, she was beginning to realise, made you do the strangest things.

'My husband didn't want Luke to keep quiet for his sake. He wanted him to speak out but Luke wouldn't hear of it. Besides, I still had Luke. The Fitzroys had lost their only son.' Mrs Harrison leaned across and touched Tania's hand. 'Their whole life was destroyed that night, along with their son's. Can you understand?'

Tania felt a mental relief finally being lifted off her shoulders. Whatever had happened, it was time to let Harry rest in peace.

'Yes, I can.'

Mrs Harrison's eyes softened. 'Now

I've finished interfering and Luke's waiting for you at the house.'

★   ★   ★

Quite how it happened, Tania didn't know, but she found herself on trembling legs walking down the gravel drive, past the azaleas and rhododendron bushes, the rose beds and the swaying daffodils. It was the longest walk of her life. As she reached the oak door, it was yanked open and Luke stood before her.

There were dark circles under his haunted eyes and his jeans hung on him. Tania gasped. Did she look as bad as that as well?

'Tania?' His voice was hoarse. 'You look . . . beautiful.'

Tania swallowed the blockage in her throat. She'd worn travelling clothes — comfortable jeans, a shirt, and her hair was loose. She hadn't bothered too much with make-up, just some mascara and lipstick. No one in their right mind could call her beautiful, she thought, but then she and Luke were both insane — with love.

'So do you,' she managed to respond.

He dragged her to him and the next moment his lips were on hers, crushing the life from her body. Tania swayed against his strength and when at last they drew apart, she clung on to him, unsure if she would be able to remain standing unaided.

'Don't you think we ought to go inside? Your mother may be watching.'

'She won't be and if I take you inside, I don't think I'll be responsible for the consequences.'

'I don't mind.'

Luke stood very still for a moment and then said very slowly, 'I chucked the bed out after you left. I couldn't bear to look at it.'

'There's always the floor,' Tania heard herself add, 'and it wouldn't be the first time we'd used it . . . '

'Tania . . . '

'Don't, Luke. There's no need. Your

mother told me and I'm sorry. I should have trusted you.'

'The house is up for sale,' he said quietly.

Tania clutched at Luke's casual shirt and saw him wince as her nails dug into his flesh. 'No!'

'I thought coming back . . . ' he shook his head, 'The memories — I didn't realise.'

'Good ones, Luke.'

'For a while I thought we could make it, but Harry's shadow will always be there.'

Tania had now grabbed the collar of Luke's shirt and was shaking him. 'Will you shut up?' she ground at him. 'Your mother mentioned your blasted pride. It's time you swallowed it and we got on with our life.'

'Tania, for heaven's sake,' he clamped his hands round her wrists and tried to pull her off, 'you're strangling me.'

'I'll carry on strangling you, until you agree to marry me.'

Tania watched the colour drain from

Luke's face. 'Would you mind repeating that very slowly?' He ground out the words as if each one was coated with nails.

'I'm not sure if it's a leap year or not, but who bothers with things like that these days? We don't have to get married if you don't want to, although I rather like the idea of a large family and . . . '

'Tania,' Luke repeated menacingly. 'What did you just say?'

Tania let a slow smile stretch across her face. 'Haven't you been paying attention? I asked you if you'd do me the honour of marrying me.'

There was a fraction's pause before Luke said, 'No.'

Tania went very still. 'Why not?'

'Because you've got the script wrong and we're not on the patio and I'm not going to let you propose to me when the thought of proposing to you is the one thing that's kept me going for ten years.'

'You old-fashioned romantic.' Tania

trailed a hand down the side of his face, her fingers lingering on his scar. He groaned and turned his lips to the palm of her hand.

'And then there's the question of a ring . . .' Tania began to wriggle against him. He groaned as parts of her body touched his in sensitive areas. 'For heaven's sake, Tania, don't do that. I won't be able to hold out . . . what are you doing now?' His blue eyes widened as she produced a small box from her bag.

'If you insist on being the traditionalist. Here. I never travel without it. Now, down on one knee, like you promised.'

'Are you sure? Absolutely sure?' she heard Luke say with a voice that didn't seem to belong to him.

'You'll find out how sure,' Tania said in a low voice, 'once we get the formalities over with.'

'Tania.' With something between a sob and a laugh, Luke's lips fell on hers, washing away ten years of wilderness. Through her shirt, she could feel his heart hammering against hers. Finally he released her and dragged her through the house to the patio. He dropped to one knee. 'Tania Jordan, will you do me the honour of marrying me?'

'Yes,' Tania said softly in the afternoon sunshine.

Luke slipped the ring on her finger, stood up and grinned, his eyes no longer full of pain, but happiness. 'Do you know, your eyes have just turned amethyst and the tip of your nose has gone red?'

Epilogue

The lawn was a stage of muted light as the peacocks paraded across the grass wailing mournfully, and the last cars made their way down the drive, tail-lights disappearing through the wrought-iron gates, and out on to the Little Chipping road.

'Aren't they beautiful?' Tania rested her head against Luke's shoulder as she breathed in the beauty of the night.

'Not as beautiful as you, Mrs Sinclair.'

Tania made a funny little noise and then giggled. 'Sorry, too much champagne.'

Luke kissed her gently on the forehead. 'Bed, I think.'

'No. Not yet.' Tania stifled a yawn.

'I promise not to have my wicked way with you,' Luke teased, 'but you're dead on your legs.'

'I know, but just a bit longer.'

'There's nothing left to wait for. The guests have gone, Tania. It's just you, me, and the peacocks.'

'Yes, there is. There.' Tania suddenly drew away from Luke and pointed.

'What?'

'Look. You can just see it.'

Behind the lodge, the sky was turning purple and mauve, interspersed with coral, then lighter shades of pink.

'What am I looking at?' Luke now affected a yawn, his eyes glinting with devilment. 'Something special?'

Tania gave him a playful punch. 'You know it is. Look. Sunrise. Midsummer's morning? Remember?'

'I remember everything about you,' Luke whispered into her hair, with an urgency that temporarily distracted Tania from the sunrise. 'From the way you stuffed gooseberries into your mouth like there was no tomorrow, to the moment you vowed to be my wife, forsaking all others . . . a vow, incidentally, I intend to see you exercise to its fullest option. Will you stop doing that?' he asked in sudden urgency as Tania's hands began to move intimately down his legs.

'Why?'

'Because if you don't, I may just very well give those parading peacocks something to wail about.' He paused. 'What's the matter now? You don't have to stop you know.'

The sun suddenly burst into its full midsummer glory as a bright red orb rose from behind the trees, lighting a new day. The peacocks stopped stalking, rustled their tail feathers and looked in the same direction.

The sky now ran with red as the dark of the night faded, taking with it the ghosts of the past.

'I love you,' Luke whispered in her ear.

'Later you can show me how much,' Tania laughed against him, as together they turned to watch the first sunrise of their new life together.